Books by Jan Smith

America Bound – 1790

Homesteading the Land 1890
Remembering the Maine
Riding with Roosevelt 1898

Norse Troll Stories:

Crossing the Arctic

**Fy and Aina –
A New World Love Story**

Goose Crossing

Written and illustrated by

Jan Smith

Acknowledgements

To the peace and serenity the Gulf Coast provides which gives me hours uninterrupted by social and self- inflicted demands on my time to gaze out the window at the gulf's waves and seagulls and lets my mind weave a story line based on the initial research.

To a loving husband who understands and accepts my desire to write and his candid ability to spot my idiosyncrasies, add to my character and plot development, and critique along the way.

The most salient facts, events and circumstances set forth in this book are the events related to typical family movement from Europe to America in 1900 and the settlement of Minnesota and the Dakotas. Goose Crossing represents a typical pioneer town of the time that found its roots in the trappers and traders who frequented the area along the Goose River, the Red River of the North and the prairie lands and the railroads which replaced the oxcart and wagon trails as people moved west. The work is historical fiction, enhanced by the actual events so documented through extensive research and does not compromise any of the truths which may be elaborated to enhance readability.

1 Jacobsberg

Three years this April. Had it been that long since she'd left Bergen in 1900? Sara sat looking through her button box at the only window in the one room dressmaker shop above Larson's Dry Goods, located two doors down from her Uncle Nels' furniture store. A stickler for perfection, the window provided natural light and helped her match fabric to thread, buttons, buckles and ribbon. "Come to Goose Crossing," Aunt Sophie had written. "I need you."

Only nineteen, she was young to be a shop owner, especially in the northwestern communities forming along the original oxcart trails and rivers. Most shop owners were seasoned men, having earned and learned their trade as it was passed down from one generation to another. The recently built Great Northern track that ran on the one side of the main buildings of Goose connected St. Paul to Fargo and continued up to Grand Forks and on, along the very northern border of the Dakotas and Montana until it reached Seattle or Portland. The prairie land that spread for miles in one direction or another was so different from Sara's homeland. She continued to be amazed at the vast acres of flatland that spread north and west until buttes and small hills the westerners called mountains broke onto the horizon. Few trees grew and those that did anchored themselves along the rivers that ran sporadically, feeding off the Red River of the North. Small tributaries like the Goose River on the east side of the village meandered on their way hither and yon through the flatland.

Sara missed home – the foothills of the Nordic Mountains north of Bergen. There, she'd learned to rely on family. Home. Jacobsberg it was called. Jacob, her grandfather, was the first of his family to move north of Bergen into the rich, softer, plateaued land above the river leading into Bergen, formed from the mountain run offs. Seeking a more peaceful lifestyle and learning of this lush grazing land and relatively unpopulated area, Jacob moved his family up on the plateau. Once there, many letters back home to Bergen finally convinced other family members to come. Nels, Jacob's only son, was the first to leave Bergen and follow his father to settle on the mountain plateau.

Intending to make it difficult for Nels to say no to leave his established business in Bergen, Jacob carefully penned a letter to his son. "I've built a two bedroom cabin for you and your family here on the mountainside not far from mine," his letter stated. He'd had the letter delivered by the small river boat captain who made the regular trips up and down the river and supplied needed goods to those on or close to the river running north of Bergen.

"What will we live on?" questioned Nels when he

first read the letter. "Can I still make furniture for people? I have no other skill. Are there any people up in that area with enough money to pay for the furniture I need to make and sell to support the family, Sophie?" spilled from Nels, wanting to leave the small cramped quarters above the furniture shop he owned yet concerned about the future.

"Couldn't you send your furniture pieces back on the same boat that delivers goods up and down the river? Maybe we could buy a small boat and use it for that purpose," came from Sophie, anxious to have their young son away from the hustle associated with the shipping docks and movement of people connected to it. "Your shop will easily sell with its living quarters upstairs here."

Sophie was right. The shop sold within two days. Needing an office where he could interview and hire seamen for his ships, Captain Morris was quick to respond to the FOR SALE sign Nels hung on his entrance door. Part of the price bargaining included Captain Morris contributing money and a sturdy boat Morris called a "dory" for Nels to own to move his family and belongings. Nels made sure that the dory was big enough to transport a large wooden bedframe, a table and a clothes closet he'd already built for Sophie. Shaking hands on the deal, Nels let Morris out the door to the street and promptly ran upstairs to tell Sophie the news.

"I've sold the shop."

"When do we move?" asked Sophie, always practical.

Not hearing Sophie's question, too excited about his transaction, Nels offered, "Captain Morris will use the shop as a place to interview potential sailors for his ship. He'll live up here while his ship is in port. We'll have a boat to put all our belongings on" came from the smiling Nels.

"A boat? One of those big ones?" She couldn't keep the amazement out of her voice. "Won't it get stuck up the river where the water level is much shallower?"

"Not that size ship, Sophie," uttered Nels with a little disgust in his voice. "We'll have one of his dories, the ones the ship's crew use to come in and out of a port when they can't dock the big ship."

"Dory? Sounds small. Will we be able to get our belongings on it in one trip?"

"No, it will probably take two or more. We'll bring the bed, the table, chairs and the clothes closet I've built for you. I'll make whatever else we need for furniture when we get there. Don't you see? I can use that boat we'll now own to transport the furniture that I make up there back here. Before we leave, I'll talk to Melvin Norton. He's always wanted to have some of my furniture for sale in his Dry Goods Shop. How soon can you be packed?"

"Oh, Nels, must be the good Lord looking down on us. Find me some crates. I'll need a day at least. I know your father is lonely. Why else would he have built us a cabin? I think you are a spoiled one. He indulges you. I suppose it's because you are the only child born into the family."

"Don't tell others of the family about the cabin when you talk to them before we leave. Let's wait and see what a cabin means to him."

Nels lost little time moving his carpentry tools and his family. The small cabin was much more than the two expected. It was situated on the edge of the river but far enough back on the slope to be protected from any flooding, very close to the dock used by the supply boat that made daily trips up and back to Bergen. Jacob had added an extra room where Sophie could sit by the light of a window and sew. She was an excellent seamstress and spent her free time making clothes not only for Nels and herself but for their only child, Nelson.

Jacob greeted them with hugs and a smile from ear to ear, behavior uncommon for the usually unemotional Nordic man. Nels, Sophie and Nelson had always been a special solace to him and the reason he'd built the cabin. Their moving on the mountain filled a large hole in his heart caused by the recent loss of his wife, Ingrid, from the outbreak of influenza.

Jacob's other brothers quickly followed, encouraged by Sophie's letters describing their peaceful life living on the mountainside. Alfred who had yet to marry was the first to follow and quick to respond to Sophie's pleading. Bergen was expanding and it was becoming harder and harder for Alfred to find good grazing pasture for his sheep. Jacob helped him find a place on the plateau. He helped Alfred take rock and form a small cave-like dwelling where he could watch the sheep from his doorway and be out of the wind and cold.

No one was happier than Sophie when he and

his herd arrived in Jacobsberg. Now she wouldn't have to write so many letters to him. "Done any shearing lately?" had been a constant request any time Sophie corresponded with him. Of Jacob's brothers, Sophie had written to him most frequently. Her letters to him always included. "Willing to trade wool for clothes?"

Alfred always attached a note to any bundle of the sheared wool that he regularly supplied her. "I'll trade whatever you think is fair" was his usual bachelor offer. The shirts and pants Sophie made for him continuously felt better and lasted longer than any he could buy in the Dry Goods Shops in Bergen.

Sophie needed wool to make socks, mittens and hats. She'd frequently received bundles of wool, carded and ready to knit. When Alfred didn't have the time, he'd sent uncarded wool, needing to be washed, dyed and spun into yarn. She was grateful to get anything he'd sent to her on Nels' dory that made frequent trips back and forth from Jacobsberg to Bergen. Having him closer would mean she could invite him to a meal and see what he had ready for her.

Jacob's other brother, Jelmar, soon felt the same pressure of the expanding docks into the area where he grazed his cattle. Not long after Alfred arrived, Jelmar moved his wife Inez, sons Isaac the oldest child, Jacob the youngest child, and daughter Sara, to the mountains too. He brought his small herd of Norwegian Red Cattle on the flat bottom boats he'd bargained for when he and Inez decided to move up the river. He'd felt Bergen crowding in on him, so Jelmar sold his land to a shipping company in exchange for the company providing transportation for his herd up the river to Jacobsberg and a sizable amount of penger (money).

Jacobsberg as it became known along the river quickly made a good name for itself. Jacob continued to operate the forge he'd set up along the riverbank when he first moved there. Boatmen and neighbors used his skills to have him make knives and other tools. He repaired damaged equipment so well that the firing seam

was usually not visible. Sophie, Inez, and Sara knit, sewed, dyed yarns and wove cloth. Other family members who came later made cheese and butter, baked breads and other sweets. Market Day in Bergen was every Saturday. Each family contributed to the wagon load that left during the late night for Bergen by cart and dory to set up and supply their stall with items at the market and to be ready for the early shoppers on Market Day. Supplies were "ordered" by the family members who could not go to Bergen to market. Sometimes the Bergen locals left orders wanting supplies from those they learned to know from Jacobsberg and valued for their produce. A different market, a smaller market, was held close to the Jacobsberg's dock midweek on Wednesday and the locals living on the mountainside and along the river came by boat or cart to barter and buy. Mail was collected at both markets and distributed when the group returned from Bergen or was held for the locals who lived farther away until next market day.

Time passed for those on the mountain. Large

assembly line stores were springing up in Bergen and other big cities, so the desire to pay for personally made furniture items like those Nels made was dwindling. He was seeing less orders coming his way and found himself restless with time on his hands. His father had more family around him than he needed now, so Nels didn't feel the pressure of being so available.   With Jacob's brothers' arrivals, Sophie, Nelson and he were not the only ones of his family on the mountain. Those that hadn't come here to Jacobsberg had bravely boarded ships for the land across the water. Letters from those families and others who had gone to America told of land in the north that was free for the taking with little work.

"Nels, you are so restless. You need to go to America and see if there is need for your carpentry skills there."

"I can't just leave you and Nelson, Sophie. It isn't right."

"We'll be fine. My sewing and knitting will keep us in penger. Talk to Papa Jacob. If it won't break his heart to see you leave, go. You can send for us when you get a business going wherever that is."

Receiving the blessing from Papa Jacob and a promise that he would look after Sophie and Nelson, Nels left Nelson, his only child, in charge of his furniture shop in Jacobsberg and issued a reminder to his only son that he was the man of the family now and needed to take care of his mother. Promising to send money for tickets for the family to join him, Nels gathered his tools and clothes for his journey.

2 Adjustment

Navigating the aisles to display his Nordic citizen papers and answering a few questions when he entered Ellis Island and the immigration area where all incoming persons were screened came easy for Nels who'd learned conversational English from his mother. Catching the train from New York to Chicago was more difficult. He reluctantly stopped a taxi who had just dropped off a Norse speaking family. Their intent was to return on the ship Nels had come on across the water. Hopping aboard the empty carriage that served as a taxi with his small trunk containing his tools and a few clothes in hand, Nels was somewhat concerned about the cost of the ride and asked, "How much penger to go to the train station?"

"Twenty-five cents should do it," offered the cart man as he tipped his hat.

Stepping down when the taxi reached the railroad station and grabbing his belongings, Nels counted out the coins and paid the driver. He looked in his coin purse and counted the rest of his meager savings. "Hmm, not much left. Hope I can find a job when I get to Chicago. I can't pay for the next train ticket north unless I do. Don't want to walk," murmured Nels as he trudged head down, aware that the last whistle had sounded and his train to Chicago was about to leave.

When he got to Chicago, he was extremely lucky to find a job and use his skills as a woodworker to replenish his funds before heading to the Dakotas and the free land. Once he got off the train, Nels saw an advertisement with a chair pictured hanging on a lamppost. He stopped to read. "Chair Maker Needed" and repeated the company name in his mind five times so that he would remember it. Entering the sandwich shop at the end of the street from the train depot, he bought a small loaf of rye bread and a hunk of cheese and asked, "Where will I find the Archbold Furniture Company, please?"

"Around the corner to the left. Good company to

work for if you're a carpenter," offered the store clerk.

Returning outside, he sat on the edge of the boardwalk in front of the shop and ate his bread and cheese. Finishing, he followed the directions he'd been given and found the furniture store.

Mr. Archbold met him at the door. "In need of furniture?"

"No, in need of a job. I made furniture in Bergen and am answering your advertisement I saw on the lamppost."

"Bergen, hmm?" Reaching beside him, Archbold took one of the chairs, put it in front of Nels and asked, "This something you can do?"

"I'd like to try, sir."

"My shop is in back. Let's see how skilled you are. If I like your work, you're hired."

Nels never did look for land in the Chicago area. Decided he didn't want to bring the family there. Too crowded, too busy and too noisy for anyone used to the solitude of mountainside living.

Days, weeks and months crawled by for Sophie as she waited to hear from Nels and his promise to send money for their passage to America. Nelson continued to make furniture and fill the orders that came from Melvin Norton's shop where the furniture was sold in Bergen. During that waiting time, Sara was good to go and sit and sew and knit with her Aunt Sophie. Admiring a design for a new blouse Sara drew, Sophie asked Sara to cut a pattern to her size and make the blouse for her. Using butcher paper, Sara quickly sketched the bodice front, back, collar, cuffs and sleeve pattern pieces according to Sophie's measurements, took the material provided and cut out each piece. Since Sophie was not using her treadle sewing machine at the moment, Sara sat at it to sew. Within two hours, Sara stood, extended her efforts to Sophie and said, "Sophie, try the garment on for fit, please."

"Sara, it fits perfectly" came from the smiling Sophie. "Will you add this lace to it for me, please, here at the collar and cuffs? I'll go find buttons for you if you'll make buttonholes too."

"I need to go check on Papa Jacob. I'll take the lace, buttons and blouse with me and sit with him a while and sew there. I should have it done tomorrow." As often as possible the two seamstresses sat together and sewed, each content with the other's company. Both were sad when the day came for Sophie to join Nels across the water. Nelson chose to stay in Jacobsberg and manage the furniture shop and his few Reds he now owned.

3 Invitation

With her mother always busy making cheese and butter, Sara spent her time with Papa Jacob who was lonely. Finding his knees unable to withstand the long hours required in front of the forge, he'd sold his blacksmith shop to the young man he'd been training over the last three years. Sara came to visit often with her basket full of soup makings and sewing. The two would share a noon meal and then they'd contentedly sit on the porch or by the hearth enjoying each other's company.

Sara would not forget the late Saturday afternoon when the dory returned from Bergen and her life flipped upside down. Jacobsberg items brought to the Bergen market had a reputation of being well made and sold quickly. When Alfred went to purchase the list of items requested by those in Jacobsberg, Nelson was sent to collect the mail and make sure those letters being sent out had postage. Returning later in the day, Alfred unloaded off the dory the supplies that had been ordered by the locals. He placed the items on the cart and delivered the requests to the families who lived close. Nelson took his horse and did the same with the letters in the mail bag. He purposely kept Sara's letter for the last delivery. Opening the door to Uncle Jelmer's house, Nelson yelled to the left where the sewing room was, knowing Sara would be in there.

"Sara, you there? Come quickly. You've a letter from Aunt Sophie." Though it had been three years, the words still rang in her ears. She'd been sitting in her sewing room under the lantern light knitting new socks for Papa Jacob, content and warmed by the wool blanket lapped over her knees. Nelson handed Sara the letter and hurried up the stairs leading to the loft to see what her older brother, Isaac, was doing and to tell of his discoveries as he'd wandered the streets of Bergen.

"Sophie? Written me? She's in America." Sara remembered again the sadness she'd felt when she said goodbye to Aunt Sophie who rode the cart and dory into Bergen to board the boat headed for New York and join Uncle Nels.

The red stamped postmark in the center of the two pages of paper that also served as an envelope said "Goose Crossing, Minnesota, America." Sara thought a minute and softly voiced knowing no one was listening to her, "Ah, yes. Goose. Goose Crossing." She had a habit of talking to herself when no one else was around to hear her. "Yes. That's where Uncle Nels and Sophie are now. Strange name for a community – Goose." Setting her knitting beside her on the bench, Sara took one of the extra knitting needles from her bag and used it to gingerly open the two pages of paper folded so that they became the envelope. Recognizing Sophie's small handwriting, Sara began to silently read.

Dear Sara,

I am sure you are wondering why I write to you personally and not to the whole family. Uncle Nels and I have each started shops in Goose Crossing, a small settlement named for the river that runs through the prairie lands here. The Goose River is 179 miles long and connects with The Red River of the North not far west from us in the Dakotas and runs to the great lake that meets the Hudson Bay way east of us. We were drawn to this area because Uncle Nels was told by people he worked with in Chicago that other Norwegians and Swedes had gone ten years before us in '80s to this area. Uncle Nels' furniture company that he worked for in Chicago when he first came four years ago wanted him to start another shop in the Dakotas. Lumber is plentiful in this North Country, but Uncle Nels still has Archbold's ship specialty woods from Chicago to him here here on the train. The railroad has just started making stops twice a day here, so we are seeing more people coming in to the area all the time.

Uncle Nels is making his Rossette chairs in his shop next to Larson's Dry Goods. Those are the same kind of chairs and benches that he made for the Archbold Furniture Company. I have rented the front area of the upstairs of Larson's to meet customers and sew for them. Mr. Larson uses the rest of the upstairs behind my shop for storage. I have my sewing machine that we brought with us in my shop along with two dressing screens Uncle Nels made for me for the customers to use to shield themselves from view when they try on the clothes that I have made for them to see how well they fit.

Why do I write? Since the Dry Good Shop is below here, many people see fabric they like but don't know how to sew. Some just want lace or ribbon trim added to a garment they purchased in the shop. Others buy material and need someone to sew for them. I've been so busy with orders that I've had to turn business away. Would you consider coming and working with me, Sara? We could be partners. You are a much better designer than I and can make patterns from pictures that you see in magazines. That is the rage now. Women bring me pictures from the magazines like **The Designer.** Somehow they have in hand a copy that was bought in New York or Chicago and ask me to make clothes for them just like those pictures. If you come, I would sew the simple clothes and you could sew the fancy ones, especially those in the pictures. Uncle Nels and I will send you the "penger" you need for your ship and train tickets. We'll buy another sewing machine too so we each have one to use.

We wait for your answer. Please greet the family.

Your loving Aunt,
Sophie

"Mor (mother)," came from Sara as she rushed to the opened outside door and helped her mother with the cheese and butter she carried in, retrieved from the storeroom. "I'm so glad you're back. How was Papa Jacob? Is his leg healing? Does he remember anything about his falling on the trail?"

"No, Sara. 'Fraid he only remembers what he

wants to these days. He remembers waking up, lying on his side and sitting up to gain his sense of balance. He remembers crawling back to his steps on the side of the house and inching his way up them inside his house. He remembers our Jacob coming to check on him. What more happened yesterday afternoon from the time he fell until Jacob came is a fog."

"What are we going to do for him? Can he continue to stay alone? Will one of the boys have to move in with him?"

"Jacob is too young, Sara. Isaac has all he can do to keep watch over his sheep herd this time of year. They roam so on the fjeld (mountain). Would you consider spending the days with him? You could still sleep here."

"You are making my decision hard for me, Mor. Jacob brought the mail and I have a letter from Aunt Sophie. Read it please."

"Make it hard? Did something happen to Aunt Sophie? Whatever do you mean, Sara? You have always been free to make your own choices. Let me see." Mor took the letter, unfolded it again and sat to read. When she was done, she looked at Sara and said, "Now I understand. I also know why I felt it so important that you and your brothers learn the English language. It is a hard decision for you. You love your Papa Jacob so." She thought a minute. "This is your opportunity to use your gift and still be in a place where you would be with family. Sophie is not young. She is a good ten years older than I am. She'll enjoy your company as well as your talents." The silence left between the two lengthened and Sara waited for an answer, knowing her mother was weighing the choices. Finally she spoke. "Sara, I'll miss you dearly but I think you should consider going."

4 Boarding

Papa Jacob was heart-broken when Sara told him about her letter. He thought a minute and then offered, "Good. Nels is there. He and Sophie will take the place of your Far and Mor. Trust them. I have been to America before to see them, you know. I have some suggestions for you."

"I am so worried. I'll be traveling alone, without family," said Sara in a shaky voice. "What can you tell me about the ship?"

"All ships are a little different. Cabin size will be important. Spend the penger (money) for the smaller cabin for two." Sara found each a cup of coffee and he shared his story as they sat by the hearth fire.

"We were four people assigned to a cabin when I made my last voyage. You were fifteen then, I think. I went to bed early. I was tired. We left Jacobsberg early that morning so that I could help unload the market cart before I made my way to the ship."

"Was the ship far from market?"

"No, I could see the ship loading from Market Square. Since I was first to come to the cabin, I chose the top bunk on the right side of the door. Cabin space is scarce, just enough room to open the door, step towards the sink and the stool and turn and face one of the four beds which are bunks stacked on each side wall."

"That means in a two bedroom cabin I'll have someone either above or below me."

"Ja. I took my traveling bag and put it at the foot of my bed against the wall to protect it from easy access, washed up a little and climbed into bed. There I waited, wondering when the other three would come. Come they did one at a time."

"The first quietly nodded as he came in, chose the bunk below me, used the facility, and lay down without saying a word."

"Friendly sort, ha?" offered Sara with a smile on her face.

"Couldn't tell. Didn't even offer his name. The next came shortly after, knocked loudly on the door, opened it wide and lumbered in, falling with a thud onto the opposite empty lower bunk. The bed creaked and groaned with his weight."

"And the third?"

"Towards morning the final cabin mate came, smelling like he's rolled in the swill of someone's lost meal."

"Oof!

"He paid no attention to which bunk was unoccupied. He grabbed the person under me, forced him on the floor and lay down in the emptied space. The ousted bed fellow groaned as he got up, snatched his handled bag from the foot of what once was his bed and gingerly climbed up into the top empty bunk, making sure he didn't awaken the snoring mass stretched out on the space below him."

"Did you sleep then?"

"Nay, not much. All night long one or the other of the two on the bottom beds woke, used the facility and returned to bed, caring little about the disturbance each made."

"Were you frightened, Papa Jacob?" she asked.

"Nay, neither of the two on the lower beds seemed threatening. Both were dressed in a good suit with good shoes. I knew the voyage would be thirteen days or more at sea, depending on the weather. Didn't think much could happen to me in that short of time if I kept to myself."

"Did you have any choice in who you would be sharing your quarters with?" voiced Sara with concern evident on her face.

"Nay. I bought my ticket just like you will. Don't worry. Your cabin mate is probably as worried about you as you are about her," came from the wizened person Sara so dearly respected.

Steerage passenger. That's what her ticket said. Sara knew her ticket was for a third class passage. "*Thirty-six clear superficial feet allotted to each passenger.* What does that mean?" Sara wondered. A postcard pictured the steerage passengers' cabins on the same deck as the saloon. That worried her. "Will those who imbibe too much come knocking on my door? What do I do? What kind of locks are provided? Do I need to bring my own padlock?" Reading more of the postcard, she'd learned that steerage entrances were permanent and not through hatchways. Sara was glad for that. She didn't like to think of being in the bowels of the ship, having to descend two or three flights of stairs to get to her cabin. Choice in steerage cabins were two – one with two bunks or one that held four bunks. Having a roommate she did not know in her two-bunk cabin was not comforting.

Three weeks later, Sara said her goodbyes early in the morning as she waited for the market cart to come. "Mor, I hope I've made the right decision. I'll be so far away from here." Tears rolled uncontrollably down her cheeks.

"Sophie will take my place, child. You need to go to her when you need something. We will write. Maybe I will come and visit. Go with God, child."

Stepping up on the board across the back of the cart, Sara settled herself on the only space left, on the top of her trunk alongside Papa Jacob.

"Thank you, Papa. You will come with me to the ship?"

"I will. I think I can come on board and help you with your trunk. I won't be able to stay long, long enough to see that you find your cabin."

The trip down the trail with the horse and cart and on the dory took far too little time for Sara, still feeling unsure if she'd made the right choice. When they reached the Jacobsberg stall at market, the items that were unloaded sold quickly. When what was left fit on the shelves and single table in the stall, Papa moved the horse and cart out of the back of the stall and nodded to Alfred. "Must be time to go?" offered Sara, trying to control the tears.

"Ja. We will leave Alfred here with the market goods and I will take you to the **Aquitania**." People coming and going on the street left little room for the horse and cart as it eased its way to the shipping yard. Finding a rail spot for the horse where it and the cart could be tied, Papa Jacob jumped down.

"I'll watch him for you for five copper cents," lisped a young lad with two teeth missing, already stroking the mane of the horse.

"Good. Be sure to watch the cart too. I don't want it used by anyone," he ordered. "Help the young lady down while I get her trunk off."

"Will, mate." Sara helped push her trunk closer to the edge of the cart and then offered her hand to the young lad. As quickly, she found herself boarding the ship with Papa Jacob by her side, glad that he was feeling so much better, that his memory and movement was back to normal and could see her off on this adventure.

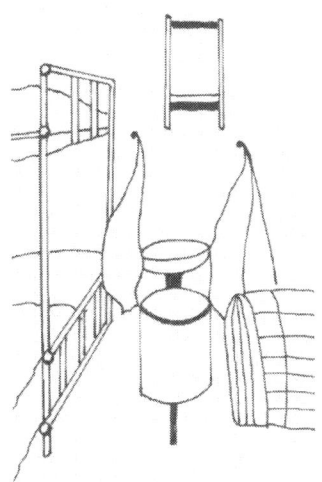

Reaching her assigned cabin, Sara took Papa's hand and squeezed it for good luck. A steward carried her trunk behind them. Opening the door and peering in, she saw a small statured, wizenly wrinkled older lady busily situating her trunk. Her dark black eyes focused on the intruders who disrupted her solitude. Hesitating just a little, Sara stepped forward, held out her hand in greeting and said, "Hello. I am Sara Jacobs."

"Oh good. I'm Mrs. Johnson. Anna Johnson. Please call me Anna. I am not used to formality. I'm so glad you are respectful. I have had so many fears about who my roommate might be. This will be my third trip to visit my son in Boston."

"See. What did I tell you, Sara?"

"And who are you, young man?" Looking at Papa, she giggled a little. "I hope you don't intend to stay in this cabin too. As you see there are only two beds."

"Oh, no. No, Mrs. Johnson - Anna. This is my Grandfather Jacob Jacobson. He will be leaving shortly."

"Your third crossing, did you say? Now I will rest easier, knowing our Sara will have someone to help guide her around the ship," offered Jacob as he gently shook Anna's extended hand.

"Run along, my good man. That was the sound for last departure from the ship before the gangplank is removed. I will treat her as if she were my grandchild."

"No tears, Sara," ordered Papa Jacob. "We will write. If the land is truly one of milk and honey, I will come to see you Sara," and he closed the cabin door behind him.

5 Anna

Sara opened the door to wish him well and found the hallway empty. Closing the door, she turned, opened the lid to her trunk and dug for another handkerchief. The tears would not stop coming.

"Oh, my dear. We need to do something about those tears. Let's leave our unpacking for a bit and go up to the ship's rail. Maybe we will be able to see your Papa Jacob and wave to him as we up anchor and leave. Would you like to do that with me?"

"I'd like that." Sara took the frail woman's hand, opened the door and made sure it locked behind them. Sara was careful to walk slowly, and Anna found a rail spot for them that had boards in front of it so those who stood at the rail in this spot would be protected from slipping overboard when the ship started moving. "This looks like a safe spot to stand. If the ship sways, we'll have these boards to steady us." Looking out to where she knew the horse and cart were, Sara saw Papa paying the lad and shaking his hand. Then he turned back to the ship, saw her and waved his hat. Sara took her handkerchief and waved it, glad to have this one last chance to say goodbye to her precious Papa Jacob. Looking at the lady beside her as she tried hard to control the tears, Sara asked, "Do you have family down on the dock?"

"No, my housekeeper and grounds keeper came with me and saw me onboard. Once my trunk was in place, they went back to my house south of Bergen." Bells rang again. "Be careful now. We will be leaving the dock. Sometimes we bump a little. We'll stay here a while and watch. We'll be away from land a good many days. We need to remember what land looks like," declared Anna.

The shadows formed on the deck as Sara, Anna and others moved away from the rail. The farther away from land the ship moved, the smaller Bergen looked. Waves lapped at the side of the ship as it made its way out to sea. Sara took Anna's arm and they moved towards the center of the ship. "I have an idea. It's soon time for the evening meal to be served. Let's find our way to the dining room and get seated. It's early but I think we've both been up a long time today. The **Aquitania** has 1400 third class passengers aboard. I'm not sure how many the dining room holds at each seating. Are you willing to eat early?"

"I haven't eaten since an early morning breakfast."

"We'll get better service at an early meal. Once we've eaten, we can go back and unpack our necessaries for the days we'll be at sea. Are you used to water?" questioned Anna, wondering if Sara would get seasick.

"I've been near a large river and lake formed from the mountain runoff and on and around boats all of my life. I doubt I will be bothered by the movement of the ship. Will you?"

"Wasn't last time. Don't think I will be this time ether. Turn here, Sara. We need to go down this hallway to get to the dining room."

"How fast does the ship go, Anna? Do you know?"

"25 knots is its top speed, I've been told. The **Aquitania** is a city on water. Besides the third class people, there are 500 first class and 500 second class passengers too."

"Oh, my goodness. The crew must be large."

"Somewhere I read that the crew numbers 800, Sara," offered Anna, struggling to breathe between words.

"You seem tired, Anna. Would you like to rest a bit on this bench before we go any further?"

"No, Sara. I'll rest in here," and she turned to the left into a large dining room filled with white linen covered tables. Few passengers had made their way to the dining area as the two women now did. "Choose a table in the center of that opposite wall and sit at the end of it, please."

"I am so grateful for you, Anna. I didn't know there was a meal served tonight. I have bread and cheese in my trunk."

"That won't go to waste. We'll nibble on that the first two days. Until I get used to the time changing, it seems like I'm hungry all of the time. Do you feel the motion of the ship?"

"A little. It isn't bothersome to me, more a comfort, like I'm being rocked to sleep."

"Let's hope that's the only motion we feel. I've been through a severe storm. Though the ship was a little smaller than this one, we weathered it well. Best thing to do in a storm is to stay in your cabin and out of the way of the crew that is trying to do its jobs whatever they may be assigned under those situations. If we run into any weather trouble, part of the Black Gang will help, those that aren't needed to stoke the ship's furnaces."

"Black Gang?"

"That will be your bedtime story when we get back to our cabin," offered the older lady, sensitive to the crew members working around them. "Smells so good. Clam chowder, I think."

"I've dug many clams. Mor had Isaac and me digging clams from the time we were five or so. I suppose she will train Jacob now that I'm gone. We always have milk available and Far loves fish chowders, especially clam."

"Mor? Far? Who are they? And Jacob? I thought he was your grandfather."

"Sorry, Anna. I forget we have just met. I feel so comfortable with you. Mor is Norse for mother. Far is father. Isaac is my older brother and Jacob is Little Jacob, my younger brother, named after Papa Jacob that you just met." As passengers filtered in, soups appeared in front of each, coming from the open serving doors directly in front of the table Sara chose under Anna's directions. "I see now why you requested I choose a table on this side of the room and on the end."

"Food is the warmest here, just coming out of the kitchens. And plentiful."

"I miss the little bits of bacon that Mor puts in her chowder. Otherwise, the soup is very creamy and good. Hope they serve it again soon. That way, I'll feel connected with home."

"Don't expect it. We'll get shell fish only the first

days or so. Too hard to keep them unspoiled. We'll see chicken, pork and beef on our menu later; some of it will be salted. The first and some second class passengers will enjoy duck, pheasant, pigeons, and grouse. Food is prepared lavishly for them with appetizers and fancy desserts," all said with a little envy in the voice.

"I think our main meal is about to be served." Sara's stomach rumbled. "It too smells good." Removing the cover placed over the plate to keep the food warm, the aroma of a good sized slice of cod, boiled but sliced potatoes, and corn all drizzled with a seasoned butter made her giggle. "Glad I don't get seasick if this is the kind of food we'll be served."

The two enjoyed their meal, surprised that so few had joined them. Finishing ice cream for dessert, they made their way back to their cabin, anxious to unpack the awaiting trunks.

Sitting in the middle of the upper bunk having finished unpacking what she needed, Sara took her needles and effortlessly knitted on a sock. Remembering Anna's promise, Sara prompted, "You promised to tell me that bedtime story about the Black Gang."

"I did. This is a coal-fired ship. We stay on schedule only through the backbreaking labor of the boiler-room crew called the Black Gang."

"Don't they just shovel the coal in like we put wood into our pot belly stoves if we have them?"

"It's not that simple, Sara. Trimmers shift coal inside the bunkers of the ship. Coal-passers bring the coal from the bunkers by the barrowful to each boiler. Firemen work the fires, stoking and tending the furnaces."

"Must be dangerous, Anna, to be one of them."

"Danger is only part of it. It is a relentless job,

hellishly hot and dirty work." Conversation lagged, each tired in their own way. Both found their nightgowns and readied themselves for bed.

"A bell will ring about 7 AM, telling us breakfast is being served. We need to be there early for good seating. I've asked that the steward awaken us by a knock on our door at 6. That will give us time to ready.

The first day went smoothly for Sara once they'd attended the crew's instructional meeting for safety. Dories which held canvas and corked vests were situated at various places on the deck of the ship. Each section of cabins was assigned to certain places on deck in case of a disaster and need to leave the ship.

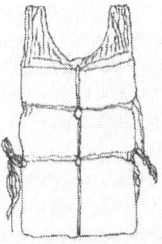

"Will this vest save us, Anna?"

"Don't know and don't want to have the need to find out. You ever been capsized in a boat?"

"Never one this size for sure, but yes. One time fishing with my Papa and Isaac when I was young, I caught a large fish. It jerked me into the water. Good thing we all learned to swim early, a necessity living near the river like we did. Once I let go of the rod, I swam back to the dory and Isaac hauled me back in."

Anna's guidance continued to ease Sara's uncertainties as the days passed aboard ship. The **Aquitania** provided a large seating area for the third class passengers. It had an oval skylight with wooden panels surrounding it. It was here the two ladies spent a good deal of their time. Sara continued knitting and

Anna read from books she found in the ship's library. It was an uneventful journey over smooth waters. Time passed quickly. Sara knew that tomorrow, the thirteenth day when land came in sight, would be bitter-sweet. Anna was a treasure, a friend she would miss. Thoughts for both of them drifted to disembarkation and Ellis Island.

6 Alone

Just before bedtime on their last night at sea, both women pulled and tugged their repacked trunks outside the cabin door as instructed by the announcements over the ship's horn. "What will happen to them? Where will we find them when we leave the ship, Anna?"

"Stewards will come and take them. We'll find them in an enclosed area on the pier walkway as we come off the gang plank. Mine will be in a different place than yours."

"Why will the trunks be separated now when we have roomed together?"

"We go to Ellis Island next and get tagged with the information from the **Aquitania**'s registry. A barge will take us there. Since I have been to the United States before, I will be sent to a different check point than you."

"Then what will happen?" asked Sara, concern in her voice. She'd heard the horror stories of some passengers being detained for days or weeks on the Island.

"You are young and look in very good health. I don't think they will detain you at all. You speak English so that is good too. Since you intend to board the train and go on to Chicago, once you pass inspection, you will get on another barge which will take you to the railroad station. Have all your papers ready to hand to the authority behind the counter."

Anna had them up early and down to their deportation areas. Bless Anna! Sara was directed into a line so long as she looked back to its end that it wound back and forth five times along the length of the ship as it sat in port. She stood in the first section of the lined passengers and waited for the barge to start loading. A steward took her trunk and instructed her to follow him. Once onboard the barge, he did not speak but he motioned her to sit on the trunk. As the steward turned to leave, "Thank you," came from Sara and she extended her gloved hand.

Surprise shown on his face. "You speak English. Don't be so worried. You'll be moved through quickly. It's those that don't understand our language that get detained." Smiling, he removed his hat and nodded, turned and went back to his task of ushering passengers onboard the barge.

It took little time to cross to the Island. Once there, other stewards came and took her trunk into a large long building having long rows of benches with piping for back rests. Directed to the beginning of a middle section of seats, "Sit," Sara was told and she did. The line was slow to move. Sometimes she heard outbursts of German. At other times it was her Norse language she heard. Each time the line moved as families and individuals were sent somewhere, she shoved and pulled her trunk along. A stand near the

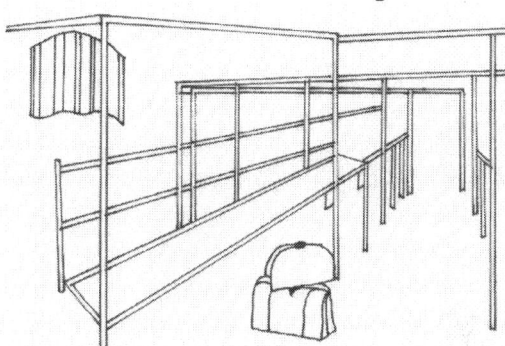

exit sold bread, cheese, sausage, and lemonade for thirty cents. Reaching in her small change bag, Sara moved quickly to get her lunch, not knowing when she'd be able to find food next. Once out of here, she'd have to get to the train station and find the right train to board. Move and sit. Move and sit again. Finally she was the next one in line. Rising when the fellow before her finished with the clerk, she walked to the desk, found her ship registry papers and her declaration papers that the ticket office had provided for her in Bergen and handed them to the grey haired man waiting for her.

"Speak English?"

"A little," offered Sara trying to smile through her inner fears.

"Good. It will go quicker for you if I do not have to wait for a translator." Looking through her papers he began the questions. "Where were you born?"

"Bergen, Norway."

"How old are you?"

"Nineteen."

"Where do you go from here?"

"I travel on the train to Chicago. I will take the North Coast Limited train to Goose Crossing north of St. Cloud where my Uncle lives. I am to work as a seamstress for my Aunt Sophie."

"Been sick lately?"

"No, sir."

"You look very healthy. I am going to allow you to leave without a health inspection." Taking his stamp, he marked her papers and pointed to the exit. "The barge that will take you to the train station is out that door. Next!" came in a loud voice and Sara jumped. "Sorry, miss. Most of the people who come cannot understand English. I have to yell to get their attention. Is someone meeting you?"

"No, I have a ticket on the west bound train to Chicago," she answered as the next family came to the desk.

Pulling hard on the rope attached to her trunk, Sara finally reached the doors outside and saw a big sign reading "Train Station." After resting a bit, she pulled some more.

"Need help, miss? I'll carry that for you." A young man in a uniform Sara recognized as the uniform of the port people picked up her trunk and walked alongside her as she headed for the barge. Seeing that she and her trunk were on the barge, he turned to leave.

"Wait, please." She found her coin purse and removed some small coins and handed them to him. "Coffee money."

"Thanks. I will," and he bounded off to help another.

Struggling with her trunk, she pulled her trunk towards the middle of the barge, worried that the wave action from larger boats might cause the boat to shift and make her trunk slide off. Worry was needless.

The barge was so heavily laden it did not shift from side to side. Tying anchor to the New York dock, passengers and baggage quickly left the barge, eager to be on their way. So was Sara but she didn't know where she was supposed to go. A horse and cart stood across the street and its driver yelled, "Need a ride, miss?"

Sara didn't know what to do or if she should trust this person but decided she had no choice. "How much to the train station for trains headed west?"

"You headed out west? Look too young to be going there alone. Fifty cents. I'll see you on the train too." Not waiting for her to agree, he came across, picked up her trunk, placed it on the cart and helped her up on the seat. "You're about the age of my daughter. Wouldn't want anything to happen to her. Wouldn't like to see anything happen to you either. It isn't always safe for young women like you down here by the docks."

Sara said nothing, intent on watching where he took her in case she needed to retrace her steps. Reaching the station, she showed her ticket to the ticket master and he pointed at a train three tracks away. "Hurry. They are closing the box cars. You'll get on if you hurry." She began the task of pulling her trunk over the first track.

"Let me help you," offered the cart driver. Hoisting her trunk on his shoulder, he hurried as fast as his load would let him. The two reached the train just as it started to move. Placing her trunk on the rail steps into the passenger car, he turned around and helped her board. Sara handed him a silver dollar, grateful that she had made it aboard. It would have been a long night in the train station waiting for the next train she was sure.

"Let's get that inside this car" came from the

conductor who had just finished punching the tickets for those in the car. "Care where you sit?"

"Doesn't matter. I'd like to be by a window if possible," decided Sara, wanting to see as much of this new country as she could.

"Heights bother you?"

"No, I come from the mountains of Norway. I'm used to heights."

"May not be used to these. The train goes through the mountains and sometimes the rail is right at the edge as it winds around, making one feel it will fall off the side," shared the friendly fellow. "Sit here. This seat is empty. That way if you get scared, you can move to the inside seat. I'll leave your trunk in the open area at back. Your ship must have just come."

"I was lucky. I didn't have to spend much time at Ellis Island like some do." Sara sat by the window, eager to see as much of this America as she could so she could write Mor and tell her about it. Didn't take long and she felt sleepy from the gentle chugging along movement of the train. A nudge on her left arm woke her with a start.

"Lady. Lady, can I sit by you?"

Looking into the face of a young girl maybe five years old, Sara answered, "For a little while. Where is your family?"

"There," offered the girl, pointing to a mother and three youngsters. "Ma told me to find someone to tell me a story. She doesn't have time. Would you tell me a story?"

"Margaret, you have wandered away again." Coming to where the young girl and Sara sat, she raged on. "When I'm the busiest with the other young ones, you go off on your own. One of these times, something will happen to you and I won't even know you have left my side. Has she been bothering you, miss? If she has, I'm sorry. I try and keep the children under control. It is hard when one is alone and they are all so young."

"She came and wanted to know if I would tell her a story. I told her I needed to know where her family was and she pointed to you."

"I'm here. Heaven knows where their father is."

"Daddy put us on the train and rode away, Mama."

"You're right, Maggie. He did just that – saw us settled on the train, said he was leaving me and rode off in the horse and buggy we'd rented to get to the train."

"I'm so sorry," said Sara and she hugged the girl she now knew as Maggie sitting beside her. "Let me come to you when you have settled the children. I'll tell them about the trolls we have in the Nordic mountains. I'll wait a few minutes so you can get them comfortable in their places for the night. Will that please you, Maggie?"

"Trolls live in the mountains? We're going through mountains on our way to Chicago, Mama. Will we see trolls?" Maggie asked with concern in her voice.

"Oh, Maggie. Don't worry. The trolls I know are good trolls and help when they can. Go with your mother and get ready for bed. I'll be along shortly."

Sara ate the last of her sandwich she'd saved from her noon meal on the Island, wanting to give the children time to settle. When finished, she moved to the back of the car where the family was and found all four children sound asleep. Not wanting to awaken or disturb any of them, she placed a comforting arm on the shoulder of the mother and mouthed ever so softly, "Tomorrow." When her head nodded, Sara knew she'd heard and returned to her seat, making herself as comfortable as the jerking of the train car on the uneven track would let her.

Twenty-four hours later Sara was sure she'd told all the troll stories she knew. She'd come to sit with the family, finding it too difficult to keep her spot when more and more passengers all heading to Chicago came on the train at the stops along the way.

"Thank you for keeping the children occupied. It has helped pass their time."

"It has made time pass for me too," shared Sara. "I am on my way west to help my Aunt Sophie in her shop. Traveling alone is not easy."

"Get your belongings together. We're soon at the station. You'll all have to leave the train unless you're riding back with us," shouted the conductor in his deep bass voice. Stopping in front of Sara and the family, he said, "I'll see that one of the red caps comes to help if you want."

"I'd like that. Will he see that the trunk gets on the North Coast Limited too?"

"He'll be glad to. Do you have someone waiting for you there? Are you one of those mail order brides? Maybe you should think twice if you are and ride back with us and go back home," decided the conductor.

"Mail order bride? I've never heard of such a thing! No, sir," declared Sara very emphatically. "I'm going west to work for my Aunt Sophie in her dress shop. She has more work than she can do alone. I won't be marrying anyone soon, I hope."

"From the experience I've just been through, I'd not marry if I were you. I'm stuck with a passel of children, dirty clothes and no money," chimed in the mother.

"Must move on and warn the rest of the passengers. Get ready. Can't be more than ten minutes or so and we'll be there. I'll have the red cap come for your trunk, Ma'am."

"Oh, thank you. I wondered how I'd find the next train."

"Six tracks go right into Grand Central Station. Each has a platform for passengers and for luggage loading and unloading. I'll make sure he gets you to the right train. Need to go and warn the other cars to be ready to depart."

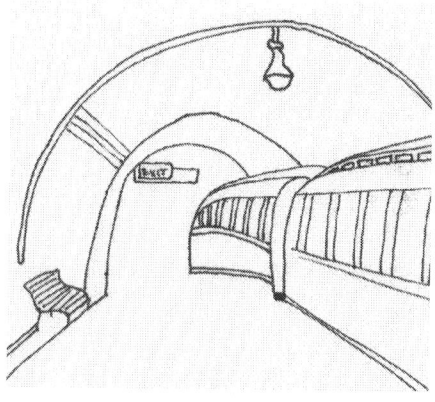

Six tracks did converge into the station house. A steel shed loomed overhead, housing the platforms of the passenger trains. The tracks split and moved to separate areas, also fully enclosed with steel. Sara couldn't help but stand in awe of the Chicago station when she disembarked. Seeing the exit sign overhead, she moved in that direction, hoping it would take her to the waiting room. She gaped again when she saw the marble floors with benches for seating scattered about, Corinthian-style columns, stained-glass windows, a large marble fireplace and a restaurant along with a 100 room hotel off on one wing. Sara had time to purchase a ready-made sandwich before she boarded the train. In the passenger car where she had a seat, she found the same red-cap waiting to tell her that her trunk had been placed on board in a luggage compartment and would be transferred to the North Coast Limited.

"Sit here, Ma'am," offered the red-cap. "Less movement in the middle of the car. Not too many passengers going west so you should have a seat alone."

Reaching in her small coin purse, Sara removed a ten cent piece and offered it to him. "Thank you for all your help and concern for me."

"Easy to do when a person is as genuine and beautiful as you are. Travel safe" and he hurried off as the train began to move out.

Unused to being complimented and flushed from the flattering, Sara looked around, saw few near her and was glad no one heard. As the train moved out of town, the scenery outside changed quickly from housing areas to homes along the lake called Michigan. Later in the day the tracks took them through open prairie and forested areas. Then more lakes, smaller now, lakes that seemed to have formed for no reason at all, not like those she'd known that were formed from the run off from the Nordic mountains. Roughed out trails led back into woods from the small little log cabins built close to the lakeshore. A growling stomach reminded her of her sandwich in her small valise, always at her side when the trunk was not. Opening it, she unwrapped a meat and cheese sandwich and nibbled away, not really feeling hungry but knowing she should listen to the rumbling in her stomach and eat. The smell of onions soon permeated the air of the car. Looking across the aisle in a seat now occupied, Sara saw an elderly gentleman casually gnawing on a raw onion much like one would eat an apple. Glad he was not her seatmate, Sara placed her valise on the open seat to her right, hoping to deter someone sitting next to her who was coming on board at train stops along the way. At intervals of seven miles or so, Sara guessed, the train made stops, replenishing water and wood. The train needed both to fuel its engine. Sometimes wind directed the smoke from the train's smokestacks across the side of the train windows, blurring her visibility. She ate and watched out the train window regardless, entranced by the peacefulness of the area. Time passed quickly without incident.

"St. Paul next stop. Prepare to depart," hollered the conductor as he came through the train.

"Sir. I'm going to Goose Crossing. Do I need to change trains?" asked Sara.

"Yes. You need to board the North Coast Limited Number 1. That train will not leave for some time once we arrive in St. Paul. We need to turn this train around so we can head back. The engine has to move through the roundabout so we can do that. Once this engine has attached to its new set of cars, then the Limited will come in and connect to its set. It needs to wait until the North Coast Limited 2 returns from the same route you will take west. Best you go into the station and wait there. Find food if you'd like. There are lots of choices. You'll find a time schedule on one

of the blackboards telling you when to expect the Limited."

"How about my trunk? Do I have to get it from baggage and see that it gets on the Limited?"

"No, it'll be transferred for you. The ticket you have tied on to your trunk will tell the baggage boys what to do with it. Don't worry" and he hurried off to the next car.

Papa Jacob had warned her about the Chicago train station and how difficult he'd found finding his way around in there. She'd been lucky to have such a caring conductor that provided the red-cap for her at that station. Here she felt blessed too.

North Coast Limited 1. She didn't know there were two Limiteds. "Must be only one track," decided Sara. "The further I go west, the less conveniences there seem to be. Wonder if they have running water, electricity, or a hospital in Goose Crossing. Won't be long and I'll know. By sometime tomorrow I should be in Goose. Hope someone meets me at the depot. I have no idea where Aunt Sophie and Uncle Nels live," she mumbled to herself.

Once she boarded the train, Sara fell asleep to the rocking of the car as it lumbered down the tracks. Unsure of how long she slept, she was jarred awake by the conductor walking through the car loudly declaring, "Next stop, Goose Crossing. Next stop, Goose Crossing." Hurrying to gather all her belongings, she prepared to depart, worrying if someone would meet her. Looking out the train car window, she was very surprised. Goose Crossing looked no bigger than Jacobsberg. Why had she thought it would be bigger?

7 Arrival

"Uncle Nels. Uncle Nels," shouted Sara as she saw him riding in a cart pulled by his horse towards the train platform. "Thank goodness. I worried so that no one would meet me."

"I'm here. Glad that you are safely here too."

Sara hugged him and then took a good look at his face. The sadness in his eyes and slump of his shoulders made her realize something was not right. "Are you ill? You should have sent someone to get me if you are not feeling well. Let's sit on this bench for a bit" and she led him to the side bench beside the door into the station depot.

Sitting with her, he said, "I'm feeling well. Just a little depressed. I have sad news for you too."

"Our family back in Jacobsberg is fine. You couldn't have heard sad news from them. I only bring happy greetings. What is troubling you, Uncle Nels?"

"It's your Aunt Sophie. She contacted influenza. Tried to use some herbal preparations but finally went to see Doctor Harem. He prescribed medicine for her but she was weakened so and passed away two weeks ago. I had no way to let you know."

"Aunt Sophie gone?" Sara couldn't comprehend at first. Questions loomed in her mind. What would she do? Would Uncle Nels stay here? Would he move somewhere else? She had little money left. How was she to get money to return to Jacobsberg? What would happen to Aunt Sophie's Dress Shop?

"Don't worry child. Sorry, I should not call you child. I know you are nineteen and a grown woman. She is at peace. She did not suffer. She slept away. Best way to go to the Lord."

"I am so sorry for you. She must leave a large hole in your heart."

"She does. With you coming, a bit of that hole will fill if you agree to stay. Come. I've brought the cart so we can take your trunk and valise to the house. We'll talk more when we get there." Finding inner strength, Nels took Sara's arm and led her to the horse and cart hitched at the station rail.

Sara remained silent as he loaded both her trunk and valise on the back of the small cart. Nels guided the horse down the main street and over a short trail a quarter mile beyond the church where a well-built cabin stood.

"Go inside. I'll bring the trunk and valise in first. Then, I'll put my roan and cart away at the Livery Stable. It will take me a little time. Don't be worried. I have coffee on the back of the stove." Helping her down, he unloaded the trunk and valise and took both up the stairs to what would be Sara's bedroom.

Sara watched him through the door as he moved

slowly to the horse and cart and felt through his demeanor some of the pain he must feel from her favorite aunt's passing. Spending a few minutes looking around, she was pleasantly surprised at the space and comfort the cabin provided. No electricity but kerosene lamps stood on various handmade tables. A pump was visible over the sink under the window in the middle of a set of beautifully crafted wood cupboards. A large table sported sturdy clawed feet with eight high backed chairs surrounding it. A large metal cook stove stood in one corner. Sara went to the closest cupboard, found a cup and poured coffee. Its pleasing strong smell helped to sooth her nerves, strung tight from all the travel and the questions that loomed from the passing of her favorite aunt. As she sat and sipped her coffee, she wondered if Uncle Nels cooked. "Where will I stay? It's not proper for me to stay here. There is no other woman present," decided Sara. She had little time to wait until her uncle came back from the stable.

"Good. Found a cup and coffee. Sorry I don't have a sweet. I don't cook much. Have taken most of my meals either at the hotel or at Marta's."

"Haven't had good coffee like this since I left home."

"Pour me a cup please and we'll sit and talk. I have someone at the shop and he will close it so I don't have to go back today."

"Is it proper?" came from Sara with a little embarrassment in her voice.

"Proper? What do you mean proper?" He scratched his beard and thought a while. "Proper?" Then he looked at her and she was blushing. "Oh, I understand. There is no woman here."

"What am I to do? I can't stay here."

"Sara, you are in a new country. Rules change

here. I have told everyone important that I care to know that my niece, Sara, is coming. Don't worry. It will be fine. I have a welcoming gift for you."

"Rules change here" rang in her ears as he rose and moved up the stairs that sported a beautifully carved rail on one side. She hoped so. She didn't want to be made a fool of the first time she met someone. Getting up, she found Uncle Nels a cup, filled it with coffee and refilled hers. When he came down, he had a piece of paper in his hand.

"Sara, just before my Sophie died, she asked for a piece of paper so she could write a letter to you. Here it is. Please read."

Taking the paper he handed her, she carefully unfolded it and read:

Dear Sara,
    I have little time left. Uncle Nels and I have talked. If you are willing, we would like to give you the dress shop that I have started over the Dry Good Store. It is yours to run as you like. You are the only niece we have in the family. I know that you have the skills to make the clothes that I have orders for that I will not be able to fill. Your sense of design and color will be an added attraction for the women who are so interested now in the fashion magazines and try to dress like some of those people. We wouldn't offer the shop to you if we didn't think you were capable. Please think about it. Know that we love you. If you do choose to return to Jacobsberg, we will understand. The stash of money that you will find in the left top sewing machine drawer should buy your ticket back home. I hope the money gets used for sewing supplies. We will understand if you are so overwhelmed that you'd rather leave this "wild west"

and go back home.
   Your loving aunt, Sophie

   Tears rolled down Sara's cheeks. Uncle Nels handed her his handkerchief and she wiped but the tears continued to come. In a shaky voice she spoke. "I - I don't know if I can accept this gift."
   "Why is that, Sara?" Concern filled Nels' voice, worrying that somehow the letter had offended her.
   "It's such a large gift. I don't deserve it. I am only a niece, not a child of yours."
   "In our minds, you've always been a child of ours. You need rest after your long journey. Tomorrow I will walk you around the village, introduce you to people and show you the dress shop. Your bedroom is on the right of the stairs. Go up to your room now. Leave the unpacking until you are satisfied that you should stay. I understand. Know that it's my wish that you do stay, child, but I know it won't be an easy decision for you to make."
   Standing, Sara walked to him, hugged him, took her cup to the sink and rinsed it. Walking to a small door in the kitchen area that she thought must be the pantry, she opened it, saw flour and baking soda, shut the door, turned and said, "Looks like the pantry is well supplied. I'll make pancakes in the morning before we take that walk." Striding back towards him, she gave him one more bear hug and climbed the stairs to what would be her room if she stayed.

8 Breakfast

Sun shining in the window of what was now her bedroom awoke her early. Rising, she poured water from the pitcher into the bowl and washed. Dressing in a simple traveling suit she'd brought with, Sara went downstairs, found a bowl and the fixings for pancakes. Not long after, Nels joined her and the two shared breakfast.

"Good pancakes, Sara. Some young man will be very lucky."

"You can't be too sure saying that. I haven't been here a day yet. Maybe that's all I know how to make."

"Your Mor would have seen to teaching you more skills than making pancakes. I'll help you with the dishes and then we'll take a walk around Crossing. I'll show you my shop and Sophie's shop too."

Thankful for his help, knowing that dishes were usually not Norse men's duties, Sara asked as they cleaned up the breakfast mess, "What do you know about the history of this area?"

"Let's see, Goose is situated with the railroad tracks you came in on running east and west through town on one side and the river flowing steadily east and west on the other."

"River? I was asleep when we came in. The conductor came through and told us to get ready to depart. With my scrambling to gather all my belongings, I didn't look across the seats and out the other windows opposite from where I sat."

"That's how the berg got its name. When we crossed that little bridge beyond the church on that trail, we crossed a little feeding stream here by the house that runs to the Goose River. In the early days traffic came and went continuously on foot, oxen, mule, horse or by river for various reasons through the sleepy village of Goose Crossing. Few traders use the Goose River now like it was once used. The Goose is part of the watershed of the Hudson Bay and the Red River of the North. The Voyageurs who came early to this area regularly traveled the 175 mile long Goose tributary."

"Voyageurs? I don't know that word's meaning."

"I forget that you are new. The Voyageurs were the trappers and traders that vigorously bartered ammunition, spices and herbal remedies for pelts."

"If the Goose isn't used so much for trading today, do the people use the river at all?"

"Today, Sara, Joe Jenkins has fishing boats that line the shore of the river. "You'll see a fishing dock

"Voyageurs? I don't know that word's meaning."

"I forget that you are new. The Voyageurs were the trappers and traders that vigorously bartered ammunition, spices and herbal remedies for pelts."

"If the Goose isn't used so much for trading today, do the people use the river at all?"

"Today, Sara, Joe Jenkins has fishing boats that line the shore of the river. "You'll see a fishing dock behind the church which extends out into the widening of the river."

"The youngsters here must really like the fishing dock. Will you take me fishing, Uncle Nels? I love to fish. I need to learn which fish are good to eat and which I should throw back."

"Ja, I will. On warm sunny Sunday afternoons, young boys elbow for room to stand and fish on the T end of the dock. Sometimes their scuffling pushes one overboard and into the water. Living so close to the water, most can swim like you learned, Sara, and are happy to have an excuse to get wet and cool off."

"Our river off the mountain is a fast flowing river. Is the Goose?"

"I remember that fast water well. No, this river current slows in front of the dock. Situated on the bend of the river, the water eddies around the dock and makes the fishing good." With a sheepish grin on his face, he continued, "A girl knows she's being seriously courted when a young man asks to take her out in one of Jenkin's smaller two-seater boats for a ride on the river."

"Don't start your match making. I haven't decided what I'm to do." To quickly change his thoughts, she added. "The railroad left room for the berg to grow. That's good."

"Ja, like I told you, the river borders the west side of the town and the train tracks define the east side of Goose Crossing. The trains come through twice a day, one going west, the North Coast Limited 1, the one you came in on. Another comes from the east on the same tracks, the North Coast Limited 2. Did you have to wait for it to come so the tracks would be clear?"

"A little. Long enough so I was able to find a sandwich."

"Today trains replace the early deliveries that the stagecoach and the Pony Express made."

"Why do the trains stop here? Seems like it's much smaller than most of the places we stopped.

"You'll soon learn that many of the bergs in the area west of here are as small as Goose or smaller The trains stop and replenish the necessary water and wood needed to fill the wood box on board and the boiler."

"Many people come like I did?"

"Not really. Passengers step off to stretch, find a meal and sometimes a room if travel has been difficult and rest is needed."

"Not much is delivered?"

"Mail is unloaded, often anxiously awaited for one reason or the other. Some bulk goods too."

"Did Stout get here? I worried so about him when Papa Jacob asked to send him to Aunt Sophie. I realized he'd be in the hold of the ship."

"He did and is fine shape too. He came in on the

train like you did."

"Why did you and Aunt Sophie decide to come to this area?"

"When I first came to America, I spent some time in Chicago, remember? When I left New York and on my way to Chicago, I'd used some of the penger I had with me to pay for meals and tips. As you know, money goes quickly to the stewards and such. I wanted to replace as much as I felt I needed before I went west to look for land. I wasn't sure what land would cost. I didn't think it would be free like we'd read in the advertisements. I was lucky. I saw a poster in the train station for a company wanting a chair maker. I had no idea where the company was or what kind of chairs they wanted made. I hired a horse and carriage to take me to the business."

"Dealing with transportation was hard for me," said Sara. "Trusting people to tell me the right directions or to take me where I needed to go took courage. The Lord found good people. I never was lost."

"It was a worry for Sophie when she came too. It is a bit easier for a man. I was hired and worked for the Archbold Furniture Company and learned to make Rossette Chairs. Archbold's is next to a large lumber yard that sells wood planking and is a good supplier for them."

"Is that where you get your wood now?"

"Yes, some. I buy from the local lumbermen who cut wood close to here, too. Archbold's willingly agreed to supply specialty woods and see that they were properly shipped on the North Coast Limited 1 heading west to my shop when I had one. I agreed to continue to making Rossette chairs for their shop in Chicago and send them back on the train going east. Come with me and we'll walk up to Jon's Mercantile which is on the other end of this street and cross over to Marta's Boarding House. I promised her I'd bring you to meet her as soon as I could when you arrived."

"You'll have to help me keep everyone straight until I've met them a time or two. Did everyone just show up and build a shop like you and Aunt Sophie did?"

"No, Henry Hanson's barber shop next to my furniture store is another story. He was devastated by grasshoppers two years ago now."

"Grasshoppers? You have them here too?"

"Worse than back home, Sara. They come in black clouds, eat everything in sight, lay eggs and come back again and again from the hatching. The Bonanza farmers were after him to sell his homesteaded land to them."

"Bonanza farmers? My brain is spinning with so much new information."

"Ja, Sara. You have lots to learn about living in the west if you stay but you're young and learn quickly. You'll do fine. The Bonanza farms are very large areas of land that one person can own or a group of people own. The railroad came and offered to buy his land. They were looking for land to build a railroad line that would lead from Fargo to Billings and on to Portland or Seattle."

"Too bad he was so devastated by those insects. I know there are eggs left by those miserable swarms that come in dark clouds. I was six when we had them come that year. Is there nothing you can do today to stop their hatching?"

"Selma, Henry's wife, asked the same question. She didn't want to leave the homestead where they'd cleared land and built a sturdy log cabin. Even burning off the chaff hasn't worked here, I understand," said Nels.

"So he took the company's offer? Was he given a fair price?"

"Henry knew that sometimes sure money is better than an uncertain future. He didn't want to sell to those Bonanza boys! They were too big business for him so in the end he accepted the railroad offer."

"How did he choose Goose as a place to live?"

"Just like Aunt Sophie and I did. Henry packed a large flatbed wagon with as much of their belongings as they could put aboard and headed back this way, away from the Bonanza farm boys. They tented by the river not far from Jenkin's place the first three nights they were here. The few cattle he brought with him needed to eat and rest. Because of the grasshoppers, they hadn't been fed well for quite a while."

"So what made him stay?" asked Sara as she wondered if there was something here that would make her stay too.

"Henry's father was a barber, owned a shop once too. He'd learned the trade but wanted to go west like me. Banking his money with Lucas from the sale of his land when he first came here, Lucas asked where the family was. Henry told him they were in a tent over by the river with the cattle. When Lucas learned that he and his family were tenting by the river, Lucas offered to let them use his cabin. They now live in that same first log house Lucas built when he came here."

"Lucas? The banker? Did he leave then? Is there no bank?"

"I know I'm rambling. Haven't had someone around to talk to a lot for a long while. It feels good to ramble. Lucas build a fancy house down by the river. His old cabin was empty so he offered it to them. Henry's first intention was to have a small one room barber shop, patterned after his father's. Jonas who owns the Saloon across the street stopped him after church one Sunday as the shop was being built."

"A saloon? Hate those places. Only ruffians go there," declared Sara with a firmness in her voice.

Ignoring her outburst, Nels stated, "Jonas had good advice for Henry, Sara. He advised Henry that many times, men come in to his saloon and want a haircut and a bath. He had no place to send them. Told Henry if he'd solve that problem he'd send the customers over. Jonas has been true to his word. Henry's rooms are full most of the time."

"So there's a bath house too, Uncle Nels?"

"No. The one room barber shop became four rooms upstairs for baths. There are two rentable rooms downstairs. Henry has two barber chairs in the front part that you'll see through the window as we walk by and a storage area walled off behind."

"Don't most of the wives cut their men's hair like the women do back home?"

"Ja. But we have the men who herd the cattle, the men who help with planting and harvest. A few come off the train and are looking for a shave, haircut and bath. Goose may look sleepy but it really is a busy place, Sara." Walk with me and we'll talk as we walk.

9 North Side

"The chairs look wonderful, and are comfortable to sit in too. You have a good supply here, Uncle Nels. Do people stop in the shop here often and buy furniture?"

"As often as I can expect, being so far out here. I rely mostly on the orders that come from Archbold's."

Walking east from Uncle Nel's furniture store in front of the barber shop, Sara learned that Larson's Dry Goods Shop was next door to Henry's Barber Shop.

Larson's sold yardage of cloth, some ready-to-wear clothing and a few sundries. To the side of the door leading into Larson's was another door on the east end of that building. A sign was tacked beside the door. Nels stopped and let Sara read the sign. This door was the outside entrance that led to Sophie's Dress Shop, a one room space above the Dry Goods Store.

"When Aunt Sophie and I looked for a place for her dress shop, this space above Larson's was the only empty, unoccupied space available except for a room on the side of the saloon. Sophie absolutely did not want to be attached to the saloon. She was convinced church going women would never set their foot anywhere near a saloon." Apprehensive and awestruck, Sara made her way up the stairs and waited for Uncle Nels to open the door with his key. Standing aside, he let her enter first.

"Oh, my. A dress form. A sewing machine in a wonderful cabinet I'm sure you made, Uncle Nels. An ironing board. A small pot belly stove to heat the iron and some water for coffee or tea. A window to sew by so true light comes in and doesn't change the color of fabric or thread. Yardage stacked here. What's in these?" she asked as she walked to and opened and closed drawers in a chest that Uncle Nels had obviously made for Aunt Sophie. "Buttons, ribbon, buckles, thread, pins. Oh, my! I'm overwhelmed." Sara sat at the sewing machine, took what she thought was a scrap of material, and checked to see if the needle was threaded. She placed the scrap under the presser foot of the machine and pedaled slowly on the foot pedal just off the floor. "Sews beautifully," she commented as she examined the seam she'd made. Rising, she went to a small table stacked with material and papers. "Are these the orders that didn't get made, Uncle Nels?"

"I'm not sure. We'll talk to Marta when we get to her place. She may know or we may have to contact the people whose names are on the slips and see what was ordered."

Making up her mind quickly, Sara offered, "I'll stay a while and see if I can satisfy these orders. I'll need time to adjust, I know. We'll talk again about my staying permanently. Who's Marta again? I know you've mentioned her name before today when we've been walking."

"A wonderful person who owns a boardinghouse across the street from my shop. Remember my saying we are invited there for noon meal?"

"Can we look in downstairs in the dry good store before we go to her house? I'd like to see what's available, so I know what types of clothing I might be asked to make?"

"Head down the stairs. I'll lock behind us." When the two reached the bottom of the stairs, Nels handed Sara the key. "It's yours, dear. It is our wish. Take your time to decide. I will always be here to talk to." He turned her towards the door of the dry goods shop and let her enter first.

"I'm surprised it is so well stocked for being so far away from bigger cities," whispered Sara with respect in her delivery.

"Some Chicago people that Aunt Sophie and I learned to know told us we were moving to the sticks! Others thought we'd for sure be killed by Indians. The train has changed all that."

"Are there still worries about Indians?" came from Sara with uneasiness in her tone of delivery.

"Not really. We see a few once in a while but most dress like we do, live in houses like we do and work among us or they live on the reservations of their tribe's land that the government set aside for them in the treaty."

A lady came towards them. "Who do we have here, Nels? You must be Sara. Sophie spoke often of you and your skills. You must have arrived on last night's Limited, right Nels?"

"She did, Mrs. Larson. Yes, this is Sara, my niece. She will be trying to make sense out of the orders left upstairs on one of the tables. If you can help her with names and faces, we'd both be grateful."

"Glad to meet you Sara. I'll be glad to help in any way I can. Please call me Clara. This Mrs. stuff is too formal for here in the west. Come back and meet Mr. Larson."

"Nels. What can we find for you? Oh, you must be Sara. How fortunate for you that she was able to come, Nels." Turning to Sara and shaking her hand he continued, "We are all so sorry about Sophie's passing. She was a dedicated woman. Her skills were needed here in the community. You have big shoes to fill. We were told that you were very talented and that your design and color talents were exceptional for your age. If we can help you get established in any way, be sure to ask Mrs. Larson for help."

"Oh, for heaven's sake. Don't treat the young lady so formally, Fred. You know we don't stand on formality here in the west. Most don't even know how to act formal. But he's right, dear. Come and ask. I will help as much as I can. I've learned to know the quirks of many of our regular customers and that might save you some difficulties you don't need."

"Thank you. I'll start tomorrow and see what I find. If I have questions, I'll come." Customers were waiting so the two left and continued their walk down the street to the train station.

The station here in Goose was manned only during the time a train was expected to arrive and didn't provide food or a waiting area for incoming or departing passengers. Any ordered items shipped on the train were placed in a side room behind the clerk's ticket desk. Larger items were left outside on the platform no matter what kind of weather prevailed.

"Early for a stroll, maybe?" suggested Rufus, the railway clerk Sara had met the night before, as they came to the water tower and tanks where he was working.

"It is. Uncle Nels is taking me around and introducing me to people."

"Good idea, Nels."

"Goose is a busy place. I'm surprised."

"It is, Miss Sara. I'm always busy, it seems. If the train doesn't need the water, the horses that haul the carts and wagons for whatever reason do. Any animals that Oscar boards in his stable are all drinking from the troughs. These water troughs are a busy place all day long."

Curious about the continuous stops the train made, Sara sought more answers. "Why did the Limited stop so often along the way, Uncle Nels? I'd just get settled and it wasn't long and it stopped again. Sometimes people left or got on board. Sometimes a shipment of something or other was unloaded. What surprised me is that it even stopped when neither of those things happened. Seemed like those stops were a wasted stop to me."

"Think, Sara. The train runs on steam. That means that most trains have to make stops about every seven miles of track for three reasons. Water for the boiler needs to be checked and replenished at each stop. The windmill here at Goose Crossing runs regularly to fill the water tanks alongside the station."

"Yea." Rufus chimed in, "Anyone with horses in town for whatever reason uses the same tanks to water them. The train's wood box is refilled at each stop as well."

"Wood is needed to heat the water to power the engine. Any baggage is either loaded or unloaded during the refueling process," continued Nels.

"Sometimes that "baggage" is a passenger or two. At other times, shop owners or homesteaders, farmers today, have items shipped to them by train and meet the train with carts or wagons," added Rufus.

"How many people ride the train, Rufus?" Sara queried.

"I see two or three each day each direction that take the time to step off the train when it is refueling."

"That means two dozen or more people find some reason to spend time in Goose each week. I know there are more people than that on each train. Most must not step off the train when it gets here."

"True. What reason do they have? Trains from both directions come at odd hours. The west bound is here early in the morning usually before 8 AM. The east bound comes through in the middle of the afternoon, depending on weather and track conditions."

"Seems like one of the shops should make a reason for those people to spend time here."

"I s'pose that makes some sense. On the other hand, I've seen some ruffians come through. Best not to give them a reason to stop. Come by again, Sara, and we'll talk some more. Right now I need to get these tanks filled" and he released the handle on the windmill to let the water pump.

Turning to Uncle Nels as they walked on, she commented, "I didn't know what to expect coming here. Each place the train stopped, the station changed."

"What do you mean by that?"

"In the larger cities like New York and Chicago, the train tracks were inside a long building made of wood or steel, high enough walled so that any sparks from the smoke stacks didn't catch the roof afire. When I stepped off the train in either of those two stations, the boardwalk led to the ticket office and passenger waiting room. I didn't have to guess where to go. For smaller stations, this station is much better built than some of the log places that didn't even have platforms out in front.

"Was it easy to find food along the way, Sara?"

"Because I could speak English, I had no trouble. Others with a problem with the language did. Different kinds of food were available at all times. I was careful. Papa Jacob told me to eat only hot foods so I wouldn't get sick from any spoiled food. Is Rufus at the station all the time?"

"Most week days he is, especially when a train is due in. If the train is late, he sleeps on a bench inside the station and waits for its arrival. He's at the platform to answer questions when the conductor steps down. If a passenger steps down and wants an overnight room, a meal, whatever, Rufus directs them to where they need to go. He's a good judge of people and their needs."

"Oh, it's hot in there," spoke Sara as they passed the open door of the blacksmith shop on their walk to the other end of the street.

"We won't stop. Eric is always busy. The locals bring all their metal work to him. He also sharpens knives and sickle blades. Makes a good metal handled knife too." Stopping at the open door to the livery, Nels yelled in, "Oscar, are you in here?"

"I am. What can I do for you?" Oscar hollered loudly coming toward them from the back stalls. "Oh, Nels, your Fjeld horse is something. Gentle and easy to have. Any chance your father would send another to us? I'd like to have one of my own."

"Can we stop for a minute, please, Uncle Nels? I rode Stout all over the mountains back home when I was younger." A horse in one of the back stalls whinnied. "I'm here, Stout." Sara picked up her skirts so she'd not trip on them and ran back to where the sounds came from. "Stout, I worried so when they took you to Bergen to ship you on the boat. You look like you fared the trip across well. Mane needs a trim and brushing. I'll see to that soon's I can." Stout continued to nuzzle her hands. "Sorry, don't have a sugar lump for you. Anybody ride him, Uncle Nels? Has he pulled anything yet?" Giggles came from her. Sara knew that Stout's strength to pull heavy weights surprised many who didn't know the capabilities of a Fjeld horse. "I see you have my sketch of a Fjeld hanging here that I did for the family emblem. I'm so glad. Anything to take away the feeling of leaving home will be good."

"Your Far sent the picture when he sent the saddle, Sara."
"Tell her, Nels. We made some money on him too, Miss Sara," said Oscar.
"Made money? Are you renting him out, Uncle Nels?"
"No. Not renting him. Just having him pull. Come. We'll sit on the bench outside and enjoy the sunshine. I'll tell you the story."
"I'm so glad he's here. I can't wait to ride out in

the country." She seated herself and continued, "The sun feels good. Tell me the story, please."

Nels began, "Each spring all the locals gather in the open area by the church and barter seedlings, harvestable grain, tools and clothing items they have, either left over from the year before or have made during the winter to sell at the market. A dance is held in the evening. During the afternoon the children play games and the adults compete in two different types of tug of war games. Winner of the war tug between the men gets free dinner for two at the hotel that evening. There is a tug of weight for the horse owners. Winner of the weight tug gets half of the purse collected. Bets are taken by three people assigned by the church deacons. The other half of the purse goes to the church to pay the parson for his services."

"You still haven't told me how Stout won," came from a curious Sara.

"Three others had their big draft horses all decked out with ribbons in their manes. Stout had just come in on the train and didn't even look good, uncut and not brushed out. I let them be the first to pull the heavy wood loaded wagon from the start to the finish line. When it was my turn, I was given the option to pull, pass and be out of the contest, or wait until the next turn. I chose to wait."

"Were the locals surprised?"

"Yes, Sara. You see this was the first time someone had chosen to pass and not pull in the seven years they have been doing the contest."

"When did you join in the pulling, Uncle Nels?"

"On the fourth try, two of the teams could not pull to the finish line and had to drop out. The third coaxed and coaxed his horse and finally was able to persuade his horse enough to get the wagon across the finish line."

"I'm sure Stout's small size made him look like he wasn't capable of doing anything."

"You're right, Sara. Stout surprised all when I told him to pull. Pull he did without any effort. I turned him around at the finish line. Another heavy log was added to the wagon and I took his lead and told Stout to pull. Again the wagon moved with little effort."

"And the other horse?" questioned Sara.

"Got half the distance and gave up pulling, wouldn't move for its owner no matter how hard the owner sweet-talked that draft."

"Anybody combed his mane and braided it full of ribbon lately?"

"No, Sara. Sophie never had time. I don't know how to braid and this is one time I will say that it is woman's work," joked Nels. "Stout's mane needs clipping too, Sara. It would be good for you and for Stout to go riding. You are a skilled horsewoman. If you decide to ride, keep close to the settlement when you do go and tell someone which direction you intend to ride. One never knows what is lurking in the woods."

"Do you have a scissors I can use to cut his hair, Uncle Nels? I don't want to use Sophie's or my dressmaking scissor. They'll get dull from his thick heavy hair."

"You'll find one under the wash stand at the house."

"And the saddle?"

"Resting over the stall boards, Sara, by Stout's stall, just like we had it handy back home. Enough stories for now. Time is passing. It is almost noon. We need to be at Marta's when she serves her noon meal. Joe's Mercantile is here on the end of the street. Any food that we need and don't buy from the locals we get from him. Until you get used to bartering with him, I will come with you. You'll learn quickly. Don't worry."

Entering the large building on the east end of Goose, Sara was amazed. Cheese, eggs, butter, and cuts of meat were under a glassed case. The case felt cool to Sara as she touched the glass. "How does this stay cool?"

"Nels" came from behind the counter. "You must be Sara. So glad you could come. Nels has been so lost with Sophie's parting. To answer your question, Miss Sara, the tray under the shelf has ice chunks on it that we replenish when they melt. The ice keeps the fresh food from spoiling."

"Where do you get the ice chunks, Sir?"

"Because the river is slow to flow around by the dock, it freezes enough so that we can cut ice chunks during January and February. We put the chunks in a small building out back that is packed with sawdust. The sawdust keeps the ice protected so it doesn't melt so quickly. Would you like a sample of our summer sausage? I'll cut a hunk for you."

"No thank you, Sir. We've been invited to dinner at Marta's and I don't want to spoil my appetite. I do want to look around and see what is available." She walked away leaving Uncle Nels and Joe to talk.

Some clothing was stacked on the shelves – simply made outer garments and undergarments for men, women and children. Other shelves held various hats, watches, shoes, fur pieces, belts, buckles and some buttons. On a side wall were pens, ink, quills, and paper. Closer to the counter, barrels of flour, sugar, pickles, oil, and lard stood. Another cabinet had spices in it. Going back to where Joe and Uncle Nels were, she said, "I'm surprised at what is all available to buy. I'll come by soon and look more closely at your buttons and buckles." She shook his hand and walked with Uncle Nels out the door and across the street to Marta's Boarding house.

10 South Side

When they got to Marta's, Nels opened the door and stood aside so Sara could enter. She was pleasantly surprised at the size of the parlor. A hallway led to more rooms behind and a spiral stairway spun its way up to a balcony where some of the doors were visible. Hearing the bell ring signaling someone's entrance, Marta came out, stopped, looked first at Nels and then at Sara. "You're lovelier than the pictures Sophie had of you. I'm Marta. Please come back to the dining room. I've made a special noon meal to celebrate your arrival."

"You didn't need to fuss. I'm very content with a bowl of soup."

"Some days that's all that I serve. Not today. I knew you'd be tired, more tired of sandwiches. I've made roasted duck, boiled potatoes, fresh corn on the cob and an herbed bread my customers ask for. Come. Sit at the big table. I want to know how your voyage was."

"Roast duck. I love it and rarely get the chance to have it. Wish my cabin mate from the ship over was here. She was jealous that the first class passengers on board were being served it and not we in third class too. So was I."

"You'll have lots of chances here. The ducks and geese fly continuously over this part of the country when they migrate. Sit, please. The food is ready. I'll bring it to the side board."

Sara ate her fill as did others at the table. Once finishing the meal, other boarders who'd come in for their noon meal, gathered their plate and utensils, put them on the side board in a large pan by the kitchen door, and went out about their business. After several cups of coffee and a large piece of chocolate cake, Marta was emphatic that she needed no help. Sara and Nels resumed their tour of Goose. .

"How many rooms does Marta have to rent, Uncle Nels?"

"Nine I think it is. Three on the top floor, three on the main floor and three in the basement. Her own room is one of those upstairs. Your Aunt Sophie and I roomed with her before we got our home built. Go to her if you have questions. She is a very honest person and will always give you good advice."

"Does being next to the hotel here hurt her business any?"

"No, I think it might help, especially when the hotel rooms are full. Jonas doesn't have rooms above the saloon like most saloons do. He sends the cowhands over to the hotel. Rufus sends respectable people to Marta. Come into the hotel and meet Carl. I'll show you where the dining room is. If you just want a bowl of soup to take with you and eat later, you order at the desk and Carl brings it to you."

"How much does a bowl of soup cost?"

"Twenty-five cents. You get a slice of bread and a large cookie with each order. It's a good deal."

A step covered with an overhang led up to the door of the hotel. This time Sara was first in the door.

"Miss. What can I do for you? Room? Meal?" rattled off Carl, paying little attention to who was with Sara.

"I wanted her to meet you, Carl, so if she gets hungry and wants a meal, she will know who to ask."

"Nels, I didn't see you at first. You must be Sara. Glad you're here. Nels has been worried that you would have trouble getting here."

"The voyage across the water and the transferring to trains went very smoothly, thank heavens."

"The dining room is this way" explained Nels as he ushered her into a very large room with electric lights hanging from the ceiling."

"You have electricity, I see."

"The bank and the hotel were the first two in Goose to have electricity installed," stated Carl proudly.

"The lights seem to illuminate the room very well."

"Too well, some say. Unless I take out some of

the bulbs, I can't do much about the brightness. Just before you came in, Nels, I saw Dr. Harem come back from a house call. He was called out late last night. You may want to catch him before he gets busy or sleeps a little."

"We'll do that Carl. Thanks for letting us know." Nels gently led Sara out of the hotel to the boardwalk. She turned in to the doctor's doorway and waited for Nels to open it. A bell tinkled when he closed the door behind them.

The large waiting room with six chairs was empty of people. Two doors, one on each side, opened to patient rooms Sara decided. The door at the back of the hall and facing her opened. A small, stooped man dressed in a black suit whom she presumed was the doctor came towards them. Nels stepped forward to meet him as he came towards the waiting room and them.

"Doctor Harem, we won't take much of your time. I understand you have been out on a house call all night and have just gotten back. I want you to meet Sara, my niece. She will take Sophie's place in the shop."

"Glad to meet you, Doctor Harem."

"I'm so glad you're here. Nels has been lonely with no family to share small talk with. I see a change in his demeanor already. Sophie had a wonderful business and was well-respected by the women in the area. I understand you have some gifts in that area as well. You're young but you will do fine. People look at age differently here in the west. Have to accept whoever comes along, no matter what the age of the person is."

A woman who Sara presumed was the doctor's wife hurried down the hall towards them as he was talking, and added, "If that traveling suit is an indication of your skill, young lady, you will do just fine. I like the flair and pleating of the skirt, dear. I'm Mrs. Harem. We don't stand on formalities here. Please call me Ruth. My daddy was a preacher. He insisted I have a biblical name so Ruth it is."

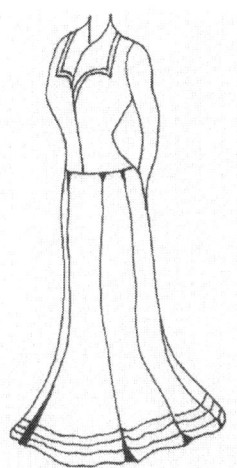

"I am Sara. Pleased to meet you, Mrs. Harem, sorry Ruth. My Mor's upbringing is showing."

"Mor?" questioned Ruth.

"Again, I am sorry. I sometimes forget I'm in America. Mor is our family name for mother. Far is father. She also insisted that I learn the English language which has been very handy."

"You have a little Norse brogue to your delivery but you don't hesitate to speak. That too will please the ladies, even those who hold their noses high."

"Now Ruth, 'Judge not lest you be judged' my dear wife."

"Now it's my turn to say I'm sorry. It won't take long for you to make your own judgments I'm sure." Ruth smirked and added, "You must have sewn for others long enough to realize that each of us thinks we are thinner and have no flaws to our body structure,"

"That I have."

"Sara, we need to let the good doctor get some rest. He never knows when he will be needed again. Is Doctor Spillum in his office?"

"No, Nels. He received a letter asking that he return home to Chicago. His mother is not well and wanted to see him. I'm not sure when he'll return. Until he does, I'm the dentist too. Hope no one needs my services. I've little experience in pulling teeth."

Smiling at the doctor's comment, Sara thanked each for their welcome and followed her uncle out the door and to the left. The next building housed the saloon. Nels stopped by the door, grasped its handle, and stood aside to let Sara enter first. Sara stopped, unwilling to do so. "Uncle Nels. The sign says 'Saloon'. It's not proper for me to enter."

"Come in with me and meet Jonas. Few are in the Saloon this early in the morning. You will see him at church. He is a good man and makes his living the only way he knows how. When you see him, you will know why he has little trouble in the saloon."

Reluctantly, Sara followed behind this time, staying as close as possible to her uncle. Once inside, Nels called out, "Jonas. Jonas, are you around?"

"Nels," came from a tall burly man with a heavy beard who had a huge wood crate in his arms. "And who do you have with you? Let me set this crate down behind the bar here and then we'll talk."

"Jonas, I want you to meet Sara, my niece from back home. Sophie wrote her before she died and asked her to come work with her in the shop. She came in on the Limited yesterday and I'm introducing her to the merchants in town."

"Glad you've come. Maybe some of the sadness will leave Nels' eyes now that you're here. I don't expect to see you in here but if you ever need help with heavy shipments or moving furniture in the shop, come and ask me. I'll do what I can for you."

"Thank you Sir." Sara shook his extended hand and turned to leave.

"I'm sure I'll see you in church if not around the village." He shook Nels' hand too as he turned to leave.

Next door to the saloon was a small stand-alone high rising roofed cabin with a sign on its door, Pearson Apothecary. "We won't stop here, Sara. I know that Julius is not here. He has a homestead, farm they call it today, near the Red River up by Fargo. It is close to one of the Bonanza farms. The owners of that bigger farm have been interested in buying his land and he went to meet with them. He is so busy here in the Apothecary mixing medicines and helping Harem with medications that he isn't able to do justice to the farming."

"Couldn't he hire someone to farm?"

"S'pose he could. Must not want to keep the farm any more. Farming's hard work for anyone and you are never sure that you'll have a crop to harvest after all the work."

"Why wouldn't you have some kind of a crop to harvest, Uncle Nels?"

"Sometimes we get enough rain and sometimes we don't. Pests like grasshoppers bother too. Out here, farming is a risky business. One more place to visit and then we'll go back to the house. We won't stop and meet Reverend Deacon. He is at his other parish today. You'll meet him on Sunday."

The last building was sturdily built. Metal guards covered the windows that had Goose Bank lettered in gold on them. "His name is Lucas. Friendly soul. His bank was one of the few buildings here when Sophie and I came."

A man at a desk beside the teller windows stood as they entered. "Nels. Good to see you. And you, young lady. So glad you've come. Yes, I'm unmarried. No, I'm not looking for a wife though I could get one by 'mail order' these days if I wanted one, I'm sure. Many wouldn't mind being a banker's wife. You'll find enough young men without having to resort to convincing me."

"I'm not interested in a man. I'm not even sure I'm going to stay here. I'm here to see what I can do about Aunt Sophie's Dress Shop. Once I've filled her orders that are stacked on one of her tables, I'll decide what I should do."

"Like you, Miss Sara. You've got a backbone. You didn't get frustrated when I talked about marriage. Some of these prissy women will have a hard time pushing you around. That's good. You'll make a good business woman in a world where women aren't supposed to be the person in charge. If you need financial advice, I'll be willing to give it. I like your sensibleness."

"Thank you for the offer, Lucas. Sophie and I have gifted the shop to Sara. If she stays, Sara will have to change the papers to the business."

"Take your time. You'll find the community people friendly. I'll help with whatever you need, Sara." The bell above the entrance rang, signaling another customer had entered. "Good to have you here, my dear" offered the banker, all business now as a well-dressed person came towards him and introduced himself.

"I'll walk you to the house, Sara. Then I need to go to the furniture store and check on things. We will have our supper at the hotel tonight. Until we get adjusted to a daily routine, I want to make living here as easy for you as I can."

When they reached the cabin door, Sara said,

"I'll unpack my trunk and get a little settled while you are gone. I do have enough time now before supper and I am willing to cook something if there is something in the larder. Last night, I only looked to see if there were supplies to make pancakes, Uncle Nels. I am sure you have other things there."

"There'll be times enough for you to cook a meal or two, I am sure. Tonight we'll eat at the hotel. Besides, I want to show you off," said Nels with a proudness in his voice as he turned to leave. "Make yourself a cup of coffee or tea. It is early in the afternoon. I'm sure your mind is just reeling with all the information it has gathered since we left here this morning. I'll be back about five o'clock. We'll go to supper then. We'll decide what the tomorrows will be like as each day comes."

"Thank you Uncle Nels for not rushing me into making a decision. I will need time. When I see how I'm accepted by the women that Aunt Sophie has orders for, I will be better able to decide what I should do."

Sara turned and found cold coffee in the pot left to the side of the stove. Not bothering to heat it, she sat and tried to sort out all she had absorbed about Goose Crossing and its inhabitants – at least those she'd met. Each seemed genuinely friendly, caring of their neighbors, and accepting. "Do I have the skills to run Aunt Sophie's shop? Will the ladies accept me as young as I am?" mumbled Sara to herself as she took her half empty coffee cup up the stairs to what would be her room and began unpacking her trunk and valise.

11 Henry

Morning came too early for Sara. She'd been awakened with the sun's rays shining in on her through the softly curtained window facing east. Choosing to wear a dress she called an "every day" dress, she arranged her hair in a bun at the nape of her neck, hoping the style would age her somewhat. Quietly leaving her room and oh so quietly descending the stairs, Sara found the bacon and eggs. She stoked the fire and added kindling and the smaller pieces of wood she decided must be scraps from Uncle Nels' woodworking that he'd brought home just for this purpose. Waiting for the stove to heat, she started with frying the bacon, knowing she could keep it from cooling by putting it in the warming oven located above the stove. Sara sliced off eight strips from the slab as thin as she could manage and put the rest back in the cooler so it wouldn't spoil. The stove heated quickly from the dried wood. The pan she'd found held four strips nicely. She concentrated on her task, being careful to fry the strips crisp but not burn them.

"Bacon and I'm not struggling to fry it right," said Nels as he came towards Sara.

"Oh, you startled me, Uncle Nels. I didn't hear you come down the stairs."

"Let me get the toaster down and I'll make toast," offered Nels.

"I'll scramble the eggs."

The two worked together, finished their individual tasks and sat down to eat. "Bless this food, Lord and those who eat it," stated Nels.

"And bless us to make good decisions today," added Sara. Both declared in loud voices, "Amen." Each was silent, enjoying the hot meal. Finishing first, Sara rose to clear her part of the dishes. "I'm going to the dress shop when I'm finished putting away breakfast. I need to see what orders are there, if any are started and what I can do to complete them."

"I'll come by at noon, stopping at the hotel first to get us two bowls of soup, bread and the cookies. How about we have pancakes again tonight for supper? That way we won't have to fuss much when we come back."

"Both ideas sound good to me, Uncle Nels. Once I see what I have ahead of me, I'll be able to plan meals for us better."

"Planning meals was not in the agreement, Sara. We'll work on that together. I'm going to talk to Marta and see what arrangements I can make with her to eat suppers with her and her boarders until we get organized here. She'll be glad to have us I'm sure."

Taking her time, Sara washed the few dishes and put away the bucket where the bacon drippings landed. Bread went in the bread box and butter back in the cooler that was a dug out space lined with stone just inside the door of the pantry. Heading upstairs, she pondered which of her day dresses she should wear, deciding on a practical cotton. "Shouldn't see customers today. Few know I'm here or that the shop is mine if I want to stay. Need to find a better way to make this dress," Sara mumbled to herself as she struggled to button all the little buttons from the neck down. More mumbling erupted as she flexed her arms at the elbows and reached above her head. "Good. Puffed sleeves are in fashion now and I can still work." Changing into a practical walking shoe, she looked again at herself in the mirror and grabbed

a scarf for her hair in case she needed it, descended the stairs and headed out the door of the cabin and down the path that led to the church and the main street of Goose. Thoughts rambled through her head as she headed into the sun and walked briskly down the well-worn path. As she stepped on the boardwalk, she looked down the street and saw Oscar leading Stout out to the watering tank. Waving her hand she yelled, "Hello, Oscar," and realized she'd been a little unladylike. "Oh, well," she mumbled. "This is the west. The rules are different it seems." Lifting the front skirting of her dress as she opened the door leading up to the shop, she easily climbed the stairs. Once inside, Sara wrinkled her nose. A closed up smell she'd not noticed in her excitement yesterday greeted her today. "This will never do," she voiced to no one. "Hope I can get that window open." Leaving the door open she walked across the room, pushed hard at the top of the bottom section of the window. It slid so easily that she had a hard time keeping her balance and grabbed at the small table to steady herself. Turning a minute and looking out the window, she saw a young, nicely statured man running as hard as he could up the other side of the street. "Strange. I wonder what's wrong?" She had little time to wonder. Button jars rattled on the shelves, jarred by the heavy ascent of a person taking two steps at a time. Not knowing what else to do, Sara grabbed a hat pin from a pin cushion and stood her ground by the open window, thinking if she yelled for help someone might hear her plea.

"Ma'am, Ma'am," gasped the same young man as he held out a pair of man's pants and bounded in the door of her shop. His words came out in gasps. "Ma said to bring these to you. . . Pa needs them right away. . . His other pair has a hole. Can't wear them either."

Standing firmly by the window, Sara stayed where she was. The young man was very muscular and seemed polite but she didn't know if she should trust him. "Ma? Pa? Who are you?"

"Sorry. Forget you've just come. I've heard so much about you already. I'm Henry Hanson. My Pa's the barber. Pa can't open his barber shop unless his pants are fixed. Today's the day many of the men come in to have some fun and bank their money they've made working on the Bonanza farms. Ma's got too much to do with all the young ones. She thought you'd be willing to fix the pants quick."

Walking towards him, she used the hat pin to point to a chair by the door. "Sit please. Let me see what's happened and how long it will take me." Sara returned to the chair by the window, sat and turned the pants inside out. In doing so she found the crotch seam split open from knee to knee. Hoping the sewing machine would not fail her, she glanced at Henry who sat sprawled out watching her. Moving to sit at the chair in front of the treadle sewing machine, she looked to see that the thread color in the bobbin and the needle were acceptable. Placing the area needing to be sewn under the needle, she whirled the wheel to start the movement of the pressure foot and began to pedal the machine. Closing the opening with machine stitching, Sara removed the pants and re-sewed the area where the two legs met to reinforce the seam. After clipping her threads, she turned the garment right side out, checked her sewing, folded the pants and handed it back to Henry. "That should do."

Digging in his pants pocket, he removed silver coins. "How much do we owe you?"

"Nothing."

"Nothing? You can't live on nothing?"

"I'm sure your ma and pa have done many things for Sophie that she didn't have to pay for. This is my chance to repay. You better hurry home. I see customers waiting for the barber shop to open." So said, she turned her back on him. He did not leave.

"M m m Miss Sara, if I ask Ma's permission, will you come to supper one night this week?"

Using the hat pin she'd retrieved from the pin cushion that she'd grasped again, Sara used it like a baton and waved it in front of her as she spoke to him.

"Another time, maybe. I've just gotten here and I need time to see what orders are ahead of me waiting on Aunt Sophie's table there and learn where she has everything stored." Stepping forward and pointing the sharp end of the hat pin at Henry she added, "You do need to hurry."

Henry descended the stairs much slower then he ascended, not sure if he'd been rejected or not. "She sure is pretty. Ma said she was nineteen. I'm twenty. Hope she'll come soon. I'm tired of the church girls chasing after me," he whispered to himself. Seeing the six or so men waiting at the shop door as he looked down the street, he voiced louder, "Pa'll be here shortly. I'll tell him you're waiting" and he took off on a hard run again on the path that led beyond the church to home.

Sara heard Henry shut the door at the base of the stairs and looked at the hat pin still in her hand. She smiled to herself. "Mor said hat pins were good weapons. I'll have to make sure I always have one in my hat when I am out and about." Sitting at the sewing

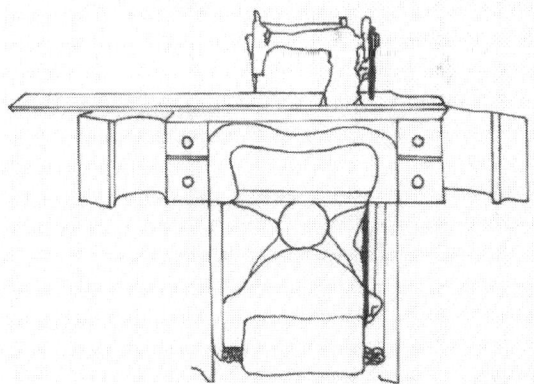

machine, she pulled the panels away and opened each of the drawers. She found various loose buttons, spools of thread, ends of elastic and the stash of money Aunt Sophie had mentioned in her last letter to her. Rising, she mumbled to herself again. "I'll need to be careful with the money and keep it separate until I decide what I'm going to do. I know the machine works just fine. Wonder what else I'll find in all of these wood boxes and jars. Best I look and see what's here before I look at the orders. I need to make a mental note as I open each of the drawers. I'll have to remember to whisper so any nosy people can't hear me talking to myself. I know it's a bad habit I have. They'll think I'm strange before I have a chance to prove myself."

Each box she opened contained one specifically needed sewing item. Needles of all lengths and thickness from those used to darn socks to ones needed for fine embroidery. Thread spools in a variety of colors, some half used and others still almost full. Buttons in sets of a similar pattern held together by a string threaded through one of the button's eyes sorted and ready to be used for blouses and dress closures. Bigger buttons for coats were in another box. Elastic in various widths for waist bands on underwear, skirts or men's pants. A larger box had stiffening for collars and belts. "Wonder what's in this little chest?"

Opening the small chest that stood on the floor with Sophie's name carved in the wood chipping that decorated its top, Sara was surprised to find quilt pieces cut and ready to sew. Each fabric's basic color was carefully sorted and stacked together to make for quick assembly. On one side in the chest was a quilt top. Sara took it out and discovered the sewed together maple leaf patterned top needing a border and it would be ready for a backing. "Wonder if this is an unfinished order. The only way I'll know is if someone comes asking for it. If I only could talk to you, Aunt Sophie. So many questions would be answered." Shutting the lid of the chest, she continued to work her way around the room, stopping here and there, amazed at the findings she had at her fingertips that were all so neatly stashed in the boxes and compartments. Hearing footsteps, she returned to the safety of her window and faced the door. Once again, she made sure that the hat pin was near. Seeing Nels enter, she said, "Good. It's you. I didn't realize it was noon already."

"You've had other visitors this early in the morning? I'm surprised. Sophie said she got most of her sewing done early in the morning before the ladies came."

"Yes." Sara smugly answered. "And I've been invited out to supper if Ma approves."

"Who's Ma?" Nels was even more curious now about who the early visitor was.

Ignoring the question, Sara instructed from her window position. "Bring that chair over here and we'll use this table. I'll put this stash of orders on the machine cover temporarily."

Nels did as directed, careful not to spill as he set both cloth wrapped bowls down on the scrap of cloth that now covered the indicated table. "Bean soup is all the hotel had on the menu today. Hope you like it." Setting the two bowls down, Nels dug in his jacket pockets and removed a wrapped cloth from each pocket with two large slices of buttered bread from one and two cookies from the other. He set both in the center of the small table and went to retrieve the chair by the door. "Must have had someone come to visit," he prompted, curious to learn about the invitation.

"I did, Uncle Nels. His boldness worried me. I saw a young man running down the boardwalk as I opened the window to let fresh air in here. Next thing I knew he was up the steps and in here handing me a bundle." She stopped, dipped a corner of her bread slice in the soup and ate. "Delicious."

"Person give you a name?"

"Henry, Mr. Hanson's son. Had his Pa's pants with him. Pa'd split the inside seam from knee to knee. Needed it patched quickly so that he could come and open the barber shop." Between spoonsful and bites of the bread, the two continued to talk.

"Get it fixed?"

"Machine sews wonderfully. Had it back in his hands in no time."

"What's this I heard about an offer for supper? Henry offered?"

"Yes. He is so big and strong. When I heard someone bounding up the steps, I went over there to the hat pin cushion hanging on the wall and grabbed one of the sharper ones and returned to the window here."

"A hat pin! What on earth for?" came from the even more curious uncle.

"A weapon."

"Sara, have you ever needed to use a hat pin for protection?"

"Mor had me put one in my hat that I wore all the time on the ship and train."

"But have you ever had to use one?"

"I pulled one out of my hat only one time back home, Uncle Nels, when I was near the docks one day when we were at market. A young sailor grabbed my arm. Little Jacob saw what was happening and came up and kicked the fellow in the shins. He yelped and Jacob and I hurried back to the stall. Don't know what happened to the sailor, but I know he was hurting from the kick."

"Still haven't told me about your supper invitation."

"Before he left, Henry asked if I'd come to supper if he could get Ma's permission."

"And?"

"I told him another time maybe."

"Well, you've just told the most available and wealthiest bachelor in Goose that you didn't have any time for him. His daddy didn't sell all of the land he had to the west here. Kept some just in case he had to go back there and support his family by farming. Rents the land he owns there now to the Bonanza farmers. He really doesn't need to cut hair and do shaves. Does it to keep out of the house and away from the ten young ones. Henry is the oldest."

"Ten? How many are boys?"

"Not sure, Sara. Why do you ask?"

"If he had a large farm, he needed boys to help. Might explain why there are so many children. If most are girls, he was probably hoping each time for more boys. Henry's lucky he's the oldest. He can be the first to move out. Is that why he's chasing girls?"

"No, it's the other way around. The girls are chasing him."

"Good. That should help keep him away from my door. Never been one to be too interested in all this courting. Oh, I'll marry someday, I suppose. I need time to sort things out, Uncle Nels."

"That you do. You've had to grow up quickly in so many ways. Sophie's unexpected death makes you a young business woman." Gathering the bowls and cloths, Nels stood. "I have to go. I've a lady from north of here that wants a table and chairs made. Told her I'd be back at one o'clock. I'll take my cookie with me and eat it later and take the bowls back to the hotel. Meet me at Marta's at five o'clock. She serves her boarders then and is expecting us for supper too."

12 Settlement

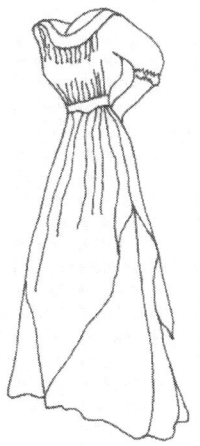

The church bells rang announcing Sunday services just as Nels tied Stout still harnessed to the cart they'd both ridden in to the rail provided on the side of the church. Nels offered a hand and Sara easily alighted. Adjusting the hat she'd bought at Larson's to accompany the dress with a fashionable overskirt she'd made, she put her hand in the crook of Uncle Nels' elbow and walked with him to the church door.

"Got your hat pin somewhere in that hat?" chided Nels as he opened the door.

"Will I need it?" she whispered as they entered the seating area of the church. Nels didn't have time to answer her. Sara was ushered to the women's side of the church and Uncle Nels found himself a seat in the very corner of the church next to the wall. Sara nodded a welcome to the elderly woman she was seated next to, took a hymnal out of its place in the pew in front of her and waited.

Reverend Deacon, already seated beside the lower pulpit, cleared his throat, stood and moved to the center aisle. Waiting for those seated to quiet, he cleared his throat again and welcomed everyone. Looking around he began, "I see new faces. Welcome to the Lord's house. Welcome to those of you who should frequent it more often and have chosen to come today." Shuffling of feet could be heard from those feeling the guilt of his welcome. "Open your hymnals to page 228 and we will sing "Blessed Assurance." An Old Testament reading, another song, and a New Testament reading followed before an offering was taken. As he handed the plates to the ushers, he spoke, "Be generous as the Lord has been generous to you. We need to buy more hymnals. Our membership is growing." He waited and watched some add more money to their original intended offering. Others pretended that they'd not heard the plea. Blessing the offering received and placing it on the altar, he stepped into the high pulpit to give his sermon. "I've decided to change my sermon topic for today and not speak on Blessed Assurance."

Under her breath, the elderly lady beside Sara groaned and muttered, "We're in for a long one." Sara had all she could do to keep from giggling.

Deacon continued in a strong dictatorial voice, "It is more important that I speak to you about giving. In Revelation, we read that the Lord will give to everyone according to his needs. . ." Sara's mind wandered from the sewing she had to do to wanting to ride Stout to thinking about what to prepare for supper. "Amen" from Reverend Deacon startled her and she stood with the rest of the congregation when the bell rang to dismiss them.

Many were quick to leave before Deacon was able to get to the back of the church to shake hands. Sara turned to leave but was stopped by a hand on her arm. "What is your name, dear? I'm Mrs. Amundson, Amelia, Carl's only living relative. You've met him I'm sure. I have a room at the hotel where he is clerk."

Sara introduced herself and looked to see where Uncle Nels was. Deciding he'd left already, she politely told her she was Aunt Sophie's niece, invited her to the dress shop to visit, excused herself and made her way out of the door. Henry was waiting for her at the base of the steps.

"Morning, Miss Sara. It's a beautiful morning, fitting for one as beautiful as you. I've talked to Ma and am wondering if you would come to supper this evening. I'll come with the cart so you won't have to walk."

"Henry, thank you for your thoughtfulness. It's Uncle Nels' birthday and I have a small pot roast already in the oven. Pot roast is his favorite. I'm sorry to disappoint you." Saying so, she hurried to the side of the church where Nels waited for her in the cart. Henry had followed her and offered a hand to aide her in being seated in the cart.

"Next time, I'll give you more warning," stated Henry as they rode off.

"Persistent, isn't he."

"That he is, Uncle Nels."

"Think you've made an enemy too."

"Him, Uncle Nels?

"No, Sara. I was watching Marie Pearson. She's had her eye on Henry for quite a time. They are the same age. She's becoming a spinster as you are."

"Spinster? Me? At nineteen years of age?"

"In these parts, if a girl doesn't marry before she's twenty-two or so, most feel she won't be asked. Men feel that there must be something wrong with the woman. Course, the fact that Marie isn't too pretty hasn't helped her either."

"But her papa is the 'pill doctor'. That should mean her daddy has some penger which makes her a good catch."

"Should. But in the case of Henry, money isn't a concern."

"Think I'll keep my hat pin ready or have another pin available. He's so forward."

"He's not as threatening as he seems, Sara." Conversation ended when Stout stopped in front of their house. "I'll put Stout and the cart away at the livery and be back shortly."

"If the pot roast isn't ready, Uncle Nels, I'll fry some bacon and we'll have a bacon sandwich. The bread I set this morning should be ready to bake."

"Think I need to figure out a way to have a birthday oftener. Fresh bread with bacon for a sandwich and a pot roast all in one day. Who could ask for more?"

After putting the kitchen in order following the noon meal, Sara opened a window upstairs, one at the back of the house, and the entry door to let a gentle breeze remove the bacon smell and went outside. Smells from the blooming roses on each side of the entry greeted her as she sat with knitting in her hands in the swing Uncle Nels had made for his Sophie last year. Sunday afternoon passed quickly for her, content in sitting in the swing in the soft sunshine. Nels spent his time in the garden behind the cabin, intent on winning the weed war.

Shadows alerted Sara to the approach of evening and supper time. Bundling her knitting into its bag, she went in and set the table, cut more bread, found the butter in the cooler, and called her uncle to slice the meat. Nels stopped at the outside washstand, lathered up his green and black hands from his weed war and washed well. He came to the counter where Sara stood next to the small roast she'd made and placed out on a cutting board.

"Happy birthday, Uncle Nels."

"It is that with you here to fill my lonely days without Sophie. And you can cook too. How lucky can one person be!" Sounds of an enjoyed meal came from the two sitting at the table. Finishing, Nels offered, "Birthday or not, I'll help with dishes. Least I can do."

With Nels helping, she was finished with her day's tasks in no time at all. Sara found her favorite seat next to the hearth and returned to her knitting. Nels soon joined her, intent on reading a story from a **Blackwood** magazine that Rufus had found left on one of the trains. The magazine had a chapter from the book **LORD JIM** in it. Nels had heard talk about the previous slavery problems in the south. The two sat in silence, engrossed in their own worlds. Sara was the first to break the stillness.

"I've been meaning to ask you about some of the history of Goose. What buildings were here when you and Aunt Sophie first came by horse drawn wagon?"

Marking his place in the magazine, he thought a while and spoke. "Let's see. Marta's Boarding House had just been built next to the Jonah's Saloon. Marta's husband was killed in one of the battles in the war in Samoa. She sold their farmland to the Bonanza farm boys and built the rooming house to have an income and something to do. Always wondered why she had it built so close to Jonah's. Fire is a constant threat here, especially in a saloon where no one pays much attention to such things."

"Wonder how he got involved in that war. Doesn't seem like a war anyone out here would even know about. We didn't hear much about it back home either."

"Never asked Marta much about it but A'bram was sent there in '89 I understand," said Nels as he rubbed his chin in thinking.

"Why did America get into that war? Those islands seem so disconnected to the mainland here."

"I'll tell you what I know from talking to Marta which isn't much. She didn't receive many letters from him while he was there but did read some newspaper stories. Germany, the United Kingdom and the United States were locked in dispute over who should have control over the Samoan island chain."

"Who were the rebels, Uncle Nels? Some of the mainland island people?"

"As I remember Marta saying, they were followers of Mataafa Losefo, one of the three rival candidates for kingship of Samoa, and his followers, Sara."

"Who won?"

"It's more complicated than that. Three American warships, **USS Vandalia, USS Trenton** and the **USS Nipsic** which is the boat that A'bram served with and three German warships, **SMS Adler, SMS Olga**, and **SMS Eber** were taking pot shots at each other with their canons. The British ship **HMS Calliope** was close to the fighting but not taking part in it, sitting out a ways from the harbor. A cyclone came and destroyed all six warships in the harbor. Only the **Calliope** escaped and survived the storm. It was during that storm that Marta's husband, A'bram, was killed somehow. I'm not sure I have all that information about the war right. It was so far away and I had no reason to be concerned."

Always interested in history, Sara asked, "Did anything good come out of A'bram losing his life?"

The United States got the eastern section of the islands. The Germans got the western section of the islands. The British were given the Pacific island chains that had been Germany's."

"Sounds like someone should have sat down at a table and talked. Would have saved a lot of lives, I think."

"Most wars could be eliminated if more time was spent talking and less fighting," agreed Nels.

The two sat and stared at the fire for a while and then Sara asked, "Are you tired or will you answer more of my questions about the people here, Uncle Nels?"

"Sara, I'm not tired. Since Sophie's death I still have trouble falling asleep. Who else are you curious about?"

"Were Doctor Harem and Dentist Spillum here when you came?"

"No, both came with their families shortly after we settled here. We lived at Marta's until I finished the house. The two doctors and their families each arrived separately on one of the first few trains that came through. Came with boxes, bags, tables, chairs and lots of equipment. Both had their offices and homes in downtown Chicago. Too much traffic from the emigrants that came from whatever direction made their wives nervous so they decided to come here."

"Coming west was better than dealing with the emigrants?"

"I know, sounds confusing, doesn't it?"

"Harem and Spillum convinced the pill doctor to

come too?"

"Dr. Harem sent a letter to Pearson like my dear Sophie sent you a letter. Harem knew of him in Chicago and thought highly of Pearson's apothecary knowledge. He and Spillum spent their days when they didn't have patients building his apothecary shop. Thought Harem would have to quit doctoring for a while or just not do any of the simple surgery he does."

"He get sick?"

"No, wasn't that easy. Hit his left thumb with the hammer. He was trying to pound a wedge into a chink hole. Thumb swelled as big as a large mushroom head. Couldn't do much with his left hand for a while until it healed."

"Was the bank next door to the Apothecary Shop when the two of you came?"

"Had been robbed too about a month or so before we arrived."

"Really? Robbers this far away from civilization?"

"Civilization?" Nels turned and stared at her. "Sara, you don't think we live a civilized life? What makes you say that?"

"Oh, Uncle Nels, you know what I mean. We are so far away from the bigger cities and all the luxury that comes from living in one. A theater with plays or singers. A horse drawn taxi. Socials. You know . . ."

"That's probably why the bank got robbed. Raiders didn't get much anyway. Lucas had sent his extra cash on the train that morning. All he had was a sack of silver. Could have been much worse."

"That leaves the church on the opposite side of the rutted road out in front of the shops that some fashionably call a street," declared Sara with a sophisticated tone in her voice.

"Careful, your haughtiness is showing, Sara."

"I'm not arrogant. I just wished the street was boardwalk too. I'm tired already of cleaning mud from my shoes."

Ignoring her comment, Nels continued. "Church was built last year. We met in homes before that. Reverend Deacon decided to settle here when he was assigned a two point parish – one here and one around Georgetown. He moved his family here, wanting to be close to the railroad tracks so Mrs. Deacon could visit her folks in St. Paul without him having to rent a horse and cart and take her there." Train whistle blew and both were startled.

Sara set her knitting down beside her rocker and ran up the stairs as fast as she could to the window in her bedroom which faced the tracks. "Don't see anything unusual, Uncle Nels," she yelled down. "Wonder why he's so late?" Not getting an answer, she stood a while watching, saw nothing, and came downstairs again. Finding herself alone, she mixed a pancake batter so that it was ready for breakfast, returned to her bedroom and got ready for bed. Tomorrow she knew was going to be a long day. She had three fittings and a consultation for a wedding dress. Finding Uncle Nels gone when she returned downstairs for a drink, she went back to her favorite rocker in front of the smoldering hearth and delayed going to bed, curious to hear what he'd seen.

Nels returned closer to midnight, careful to make as little noise as possible, opened the door and saw her still curled in the chair by the hearth. Walking towards her, he rested his hand on her shoulder and said, "Sara, you need to go to bed. It is late, I know you need to be up early or you wouldn't have mixed the pancake batter for morning that I see on the cupboard."

Rubbing her eyes and untangling her hair that had come loose from its bun at the back of her neck, she uncurled her feet from under her, looked at him with half-sleepy eyes and said, "What did you find out?"

"Train got delayed up west of here near Georgetown where the Goose meets the Red River that flows north. A log jam on the Red broke loose and flooded the tracks so the train had to wait until the water was diverted."

"That's why the fineries that Aunt Sophie ordered from the Hudson Bay Company at Grand Forks haven't come."

"Better plan ahead. If we get a heavy snow this winter or if we get lots of rain, that area floods quickly. The land is flat and water has no place to go. Needs to evaporate."

"Too much for me to think about tonight. Made the batter for pancakes for you," she reminded him. "If you have time, bring one to me after you've had your breakfast. I'll reheat it on the little pot belly stove. It'll satisfy me until I am done for the day and can make the chicken I bartered for when I made Alicia's confirmation dress.

13 Customers

Goose Crossing finally felt like home to Sara. It'd only been three months but Uncle Nels' introductions and tour had made the adjustment to living in the community much easier for her than she'd thought it would be. Each time she contacted the person to tell him or her that she'd completed the order that had been left with Aunt Sophie, she received praise for her workmanship. Other orders followed quickly. Her small stash of money she had made and the cash Aunt Sophie had left her grew enough so that she went to see Lucas at the bank.

Entering the bank, Sara saw he was not busy at his desk placed to the side of the tellers' cages, so she walked towards him. "Mr. Lucas, could I speak with you please?"

"Of course, Miss Sara. Please be seated. What can I help you with? Need to borrow some money?"

"No, thank goodness. I need to deposit some money. How do I go about doing that?"

"Your business has been good. I've heard many fine compliments about your work and work ethics." Opening the ledger beside him, he went to a blank page and wrote her name. "I will need the name of a family member as well."

"Please put Uncle Nels' name on the ledger. I don't have any other family members in America." As she spoke, she took out a large leather sack from her valise and handed it to Lucas. "This is the amount I want to put in your bank, Mr. Lucas."

Lucas carefully counted the few gold pieces first, made a notation and then counted the silver in front of him.

"I count $102.00."

"That's what I had tallied too, Mr. Lucas. If I should need any of that money, how do I get it? I've never had an account before."

"You come and ask me and I will give you the money and deduct it from your ledger page here. It's that simple."

"Thank you for your time and your help. I will be on my way. I have a wedding dress to finish."

"May I ask whose dress you are making?"

"Marie Pearson. You must know her."

"And so do most of the young men in the area. Glad to see she's marrying. Hope she got someone suitable and not just someone off the train."

"Actually, it is someone off the train from west of here, I understand. She answered an advertisement in a newspaper that she in some way saw. Her mother was quick to say that he's one of the rich Bonanza farmers to the west of us here. Hope it works out well for both of them. I must go. I don't want her waiting for me."

"No, you don't. She can spread more bad news faster than anyone I know."

Rushing back to her shop, Sara was just in time. The Pearsons came across the street and ascended the steps up to her shop not far behind her. Sara set her valise down near her sewing machine and reached for the dress hanging close by to have it in hand as Marie and Mrs. Pearson entered.

"Is it ready?" questioned Marie in a stern voice. "I want to make sure it is as elegant as the drawings you made."

"I finished the embroidery last night. I hope it meets with your approval from the sketches that I did for you, Miss Marie."

Taking what seemed like hours of time to Sara, she and her mother examined the work on the bodice and the skirt. Mrs. Pearson was the first to speak. "When did you learn such delicate embroidery stitches?"

"My Mor, excuse me, my mother taught me at a very young age. She was also insistent that my brother Eric and I learn to speak English." Realizing she was rambling on in nervousness, she stopped and waited.

"You do exquisite work, my dear. If it fits as well as the garment looks, Marie will look beautiful on her wedding day. Put it on dear. Let's see if the fit is good."

Marie took the dress with a little huff in her movements, wanting to make Sara feel as uncomfortable as possible. "We'll see," and she stepped behind the screen.

Time seemed to crawl for Sara. She hoped that she'd made the dress according to all the measurements she'd taken. To have to redo any of the embroidery if she had to alter the dress would not be easy. When Marie stepped out for them to see, Sara let out a sigh of relief. It fit her like a glove.

"Turn around slowly please. You are so beautiful, Marie. Myron can't help but be pleased. Let me pay you Sara for your workmanship. I don't see any need for alteration. Hurry and change, Marie. We have to meet with Jon at the Mercantile and order food for the dinner."

Just as the two left Sara and descended the stairs to the boardwalk, loud thumping sounds echoed in the stairwell. "Oh, sorry Miss Marie. Didn't mean to knock your hat off kilter with my package."

"Henry, you are the biggest nuisance I know in Goose. You are such a klutz. I'm so glad I'll be marrying and not need to deal with the likes of you," announced Marie to the person she'd not long ago tried so hard to make notice her.

"Congratulations, Miss Marie. I know Myron very well. I wish him luck too. He'll probably need it." Turning quickly, he bounded up the rest of the stairs and through the open door finding Sara by the window with her trusted hat pin in hand, trying hard not to smile.

"Miss Sara, sorry for the noise. I had a confrontation with the Pearson ladies. I'm sure you heard." He held his head down and then took a peek at Sara. The two giggled, each knowing that the bump had been intentional.

"Do you really know this Myron person that she is to marry, Henry?"

"I do. He's my Pa's age, give or take ten years. Marie will be his third wife. He's worn out two others having children. I think this time he's met his match. I do wish him luck."

"What's in your package this time, Henry? More of your Pa's pants?"

"No, Ma sent for material from **Sears Roebuck** catalogue. Came in the mail yesterday. My sister Marie needs a confirmation dress and Marie wants you to make it for her. Ma can sew but Ann's insistent you make it. She is sure you'll make it look fancier than Ma could."

"I have other orders but they are not as pressing as this confirmation dress. Today is Tuesday. Sunday is Confirmation Sunday. Did your mother send along measurements?"

"She put a piece of paper in the bag and told me not to lose it. I saw numbers on it when she stuck it in the bag."

As Sara opened the bag and took out a fine white embroidered linen fabric, a piece of paper fell to the floor. Reacting quickly, Henry moved to retrieve it as Sara knelt to do the same. Both landed hard on their backsides on the floor. Sara was quick to cover her ankles with her skirt and tried to rise. Confusion ensued. Henry tried to help Sara and she tried to be ladylike in her efforts. Finally, he came behind her, place his hands around her waist and set her on her feet. Her cheeks flushed with embarrassment.

Bowing his head again, he spoke. "I know that was not a gentlemanly thing to do, Sara. I have better manners than that. I was only trying to help." Reaching for the piece of paper still on the floor in front of them, he grasped it and scanned its contents. Looks like this must be Ann's measurements" and handed the paper to her. "I'll be going and leave you to your sewing. Hope you're not hurt from our collision." The steps thundered as he made his way down.

14 Trouble

Sara went to the window to close it before she went home for the night and sensed something important had happened here in Goose. As she looked down each side of the street and south towards Marta's Boarding House and Joe's Mercantile, she saw more men milling around in front of the stores on the boardwalk than she'd ever seen before. Because it was soon supper time and she was late in leaving her shop, she hurried home. Some of the men stood leaning on their rifles. Others had guns belted to their waists. Her determined walk became close to a run as she made her way through the gatherings and home. Once inside, she thought about latching the door from the inside and finally decided to do so, hoping Uncle Nels would come home soon.

Removing her shawl and hanging it on the hook by the door, she placed the sewing she needed to work on onto the table by the hearth and headed into the kitchen. A note hung on the nail on the pantry door. Sara found it when she walked over to the cooler to find some kind of meat that she could use to make a quick supper. "Uncle Nels must have gone hunting. Said he'd leave me a note if he got anything," she mumbled to herself as she unfolded the small scrap of paper.

"No grouse today but caught a nice pike. Cleaned and cut. Ready to fry. Home about 5. U.N."

Setting the note aside, Sara opened the cooler, found the fish and a kettle of potatoes peeled and ready to boil. Fresh peas in their pods he'd picked from the garden were inside in another bowl. "That's why I love him so. He isn't afraid to do woman's work." She quickly busied herself, realizing it was soon five o'clock and he would be home and as hungry as she was. Opening one of the lids over a burner on the stove, she stirred the embers and stoked the smolderings with kindling, not wanting to make the fire blaze. Setting the potato kettle on top of that burner cover, she returned to the bowl of peas and shelled them. Filling a smaller pot half full of water, Sara put this pot on a covered burner located behind the potatoes and waited for it to boil so she could add the peas. As she turned to take two plates and a platter out of the cupboard, the door rattled and her name was called. "I'll be right there," and she moved to unlatch the door.

"Sara, you must have heard the news or you wouldn't have the door latched," spoke Uncle Nels as he came into the house, knowing that he'd find Sara preparing supper.

"What news?"

"That's why I'm late. Some of us were talking and we think we need a constable. Jonas would be a good choice. He is a big man and few argue with him when he lays down the law in his saloon. We all know his temper. Not sure newcomers would be as easily convinced but we need someone. Probably need a place to put the culprits too until a circuit judge can come and hold court."

"What happened to stir all this fuss for law and order here? I've not heard any noise or seen any unfriendly looking characters." Sara felt like a nosy neighbor and was sure her nose stuck out like Pinocchio's!

"Oscar had a horse and cart stolen from his Livery Stable sometime over night. Another boarded horse had been let out of its stall but not stolen. I'm missing a long heavy rope too. He thinks it happened early this morning. Oscar found the horse loose by the water tank and took it back to the empty stall. His favorite delivery cart was gone. When he saw what had happened, he took an extra saddled horse with him and went to the saloon and asked Jonas to come with him to look for the culprits, knowing there'd be little saloon business so early in the morning. Rain left a good trail for them to follow. Others who were up early joined them and they followed the trail of the cart. Found it and the horse tied to that big oak tree that stands next to the dock down by the river. Jenkin's boats were not disturbed."

"Horse fine?"

"Still harnessed, Sara. Stood grazing on the fresh grass. Cart was a different story. Looks like someone took the side rails off and some of the bed out. Jonas thinks they made a raft out of the planking, using my stolen rope to tie the planks together."

"Anything else missing?"

"Don't think so. No one's reported that they've lost anything when they've come to the Mercantile. Jon's usually first to hear such news or Rufus when they come for mail. Might be too early yet. Few know about what happened."

"Glad they didn't take Stout. I should ride him more. If anything happened to him, I'd really miss him. He's a part of my connection to Jacobsberg."

Two days passed. Trains came and left and life went on as before in Goose Crossing. Oscar rebuilt his cart from the wood that Nels was not going to use. Not knowing who had come through Goose and what the reason was for stealing the cart and for building the raft made some uneasy. Rufus' explanation of the culprits made sense. He hadn't seen them but he'd found a bundle of men's clothes wrapped in a long sleeved shirt and tied so that the bundle would fit on a heavy stick for a handle to be thrown over the shoulder. He was sure the men were hobos who came into the station, hooking a ride in an empty boxcar on the train and needing to go south from here. Idea seemed logical. Train tracks run east and west from Goose. To get downriver and south, a raft of some sort was needed. Oscar had forgotten to put his cart away in his stable so it was tempting to use.

Jon hung a notice in his Mercantile, the bank, hotel, and the saloon announcing a meeting to elect a constable. Few took the time to attend, seeing little need for law and order. Those attending appointed Jonas as constable and gave him the authority to arrest anyone who did not keep to the law. Jonas wondered what he was to do if he arrested someone. Goose had no jail to put any culprits in to await the circuit judge's infrequent appearance when he rode through to settle other problems elsewhere. Nor did he pack a pistol like so many of the cowboys did.

The day after the robbery, the train whistle blew announcing its arrival. The day was blistering hot. Hoping for a breeze, Sara sat and looked down from her seat at the window and watched as Jonas, Jon and Uncle Nels with Stout harnessed to a cart headed to the platform to meet the train. "Good," mumbled Sara to herself, satisfied she'd learn any important news from her uncle later when they both got home. Seeing no one step down from the train to the platform, Sara continued to work the embroidery pattern Mrs. Pearson had insisted be done on the baptismal gown she'd ordered. "It'll be our first grandchild," she'd told Sara. "Marie will make such a good mother if she ever has our first grandchild." Sara wondered if Marie even had a choice about motherhood being the third wife of a Bonanza farmer whose first two wives had died and he already had a passel of children by them.

    Loud honking startled Sara and made her prick her finger with the needle. To be sure no blood got on the garment, Sara held her finger in the air and looked out. A huge flock of geese flew over the rooftops of the hotel and saloon. Gun shots were heard and the geese scattered in all directions, not wanting to risk a stop to forage for food in the lush, green heads of winter wheat that flapped in the breeze. Sara watched them regroup and head north. She longed for the freedom the geese had and wished she had the same. With Sophie gone, Sara had full responsibility of ordering material and findings, meeting customers, and making what was ordered, always aware of one deadline or another when a garment had to be done. The door opened below and brought her back to reality. "Wonder who that might be," declared Sara as she sat waiting by the machine.

    "Sara. Are you upstairs?" came from the voice at the base of the stairs that she recognized as Nels'.

    "I'm here. Need me to come down?" offered Sara as she went to the head of the stairs and railing that lead from her shop to the street below.

"No. The shipment that Sophie ordered from the **Sears Roebuck** Catalogue when she knew you were coming is finally here," came echoing up the stairwell. Ascending, Nels continued, "I remember her saying you would need some fineries and she wanted to be sure they were available. You've already discovered Larson's Mercantile has little choice in buttons, buckles, and trims. With Sophie's getting sick and passing so quickly and you arriving shortly after, I forgot that she'd placed the order. The flooding of the Goose delayed it, I guess. Where shall I set this crate?"

"Here by my feet. I'll need to see what's in the shipment so I don't order any duplicates," directed Sara who sat in her favorite chair by the window.

"I'll bring up the other crates," offered Nels and he went back down the stairs to the boardwalk in front of Larson's where the horse stood patiently tied at the rail, hitched to the small wagon loaded with crates of all sizes.

"Crates? He said crates. I wonder how big they are. What could she have ordered? Where will I put the supplies? How will I pay for them?" Questions flooded Sara's mind as she moved to make what room she could in an already crowded shop. She was glad it was closing time and that any customers had probably come and gone.

Finishing his unloading task, Nels hugged Sara and headed for the stairs. "Don't worry about fixing a meal. I will stop at the hotel and have a bowl of soup. In fact, why don't you come with me? Opening the crates can wait for a little while."

"I need to pay you for all of the fineries. Let's talk here about how I can do that before we leave the shop. I'll need to go to Lucas and get money out of the bank. We don't need other ears listening."

"Sara, having you here is a comfort. I'm sure our

lives will change as the days go by. You'll probably find someone and need to start a home of your own. Sophie paid for the supplies when she ordered them. I have no bill to pay. You fixing an evening meal now and then and keeping the house in order is fair payment."

Shaking her head and determined to do what was right, she continued with a blush on her face, "Can I continue to live in your house? Is it proper? It would have been fine when Aunt Sophie was alive. Won't there be gossip?"

"As I've told you before, in the old country, there would be. Here in the Wild West as so many have labeled this area, less stress is placed on where one lives. Most are concerned that there is a roof of some sort to live under. We will be fine. Come, let's have that soup."

Sara took her shawl off its hook by the door, wrapped it around her shoulders and followed Nels down the stairs, locking the door behind herself. Reaching the boardwalk, the two headed across the rutted dirt street to the hotel. The hotel dining room was busy. Nels saw a small table in the corner behind the stairs that lead to the rooms above. "That corner spot under the stairs should be just fine, Sara. I'll go with you over there and then I'll order our soup from Carl."

Walking to where Nels had pointed, Sara was stopped by one of her most wealthy and regular customers, Miss Lily. Sara was not sure that her name fit her very well, convinced she was more a thorny rose. "Hello, Miss Lily."

"Sara, dear. Glad to see you. Out for an evening stroll?" offered Lily in a velvety silk voice.

"Uncle Nels just unloaded crates of fineries Aunt Sophie ordered, expecting me to come and work with her. I am anxious to see what she ordered before her passing. He offered to buy each of us a bowl of soup so I wouldn't have to make the evening meal, knowing I'd be too curious to wait until morning to begin unpacking."

"We are so sorry for Sophie's passing. She'll be missed in the community," said Lily's companion at table, Mrs. Primrose.

Lily nodded her head. "We do hope that you will stay. A dressmaker is sorely needed in a place like this so far from anything."

"I will stay for a while. Uncle Nels has been so kind. Aunt Sophie's shoes will be hard to fill." Finding herself the curiosity piece left her conscience in a shambles. Excusing herself, she went to where Nels was waiting to hold her chair for her at a little table meant for two. Seated and taking the napkin out from under the utensils, Sara became aware of another pair of ladies across and to the left of their table who had stopped conversing with each other and stared at her. Sara was not a frequent visitor of the hotel and rarely ate in the dining room. When she wanted something, she came to the hotel, ordered what she wanted from Carl at the registration desk and waited until it was brought to her. When she needed to continue working in order to complete someone's purchase of a garment, she would take the food back to her upstairs sewing room, sit at her chair that faced the street and have her meal. The window provided ample opportunity to see the townsfolk carry on business.

Nels came with the bowls of soup, bread and the cookies, set one of each in front of Sara, and went around the small table to pull out his chair to sit opposite her. Noticing the glazed over look in her eyes, he spoke with concern in his voice. "Sara. Sara, is there something wrong? You seem so far away."

"Sorry, Uncle Nels. The two ladies to the left of

us keep staring this way. They make me uncomfortable." Time passed quietly as the two enjoyed the hot soup, bread and their cookies. Out of curiosity, Sara asked, "How is Stout? It's a shame Aunt Sophie didn't get a chance to ride her favorite Fjord horse very much."

"You need to ride Stout. He doesn't like men, I'm convinced. Stout let Nelson ride him when he herded the cattle from one feeding place on the mountain back home to another. He and you were the only two he wouldn't try and toss off."

"Why do you say I should ride him, Uncle Nels? Since you feed and water him, I'd think he'd like you."

"He nips at my ankles any time I am close, even when I am feeding him."

"I suppose I do need to do more than sew," declared Sara. "I'll make a point of visiting his stall each day and ride him as often as I can. That ought to stir up the ladies like Miss Lily over there. He's never been ridden side saddle style. I'll have to put on my trousers, tuck my hair under my hat and hope that I'm not seen by the prim and proper sort."

Taking out his coin purse, Nels counted out the correct change for their meals, placed the money near his plate, stood and ushered Sara out the door. Both groups of ladies sat silently and watched their departure.

Loud piano music floated down the street from the saloon's open doors as the two stepped on the boardwalk outside the hotel. Nels counted six horses hitched to the rail. When he and Sara crossed the street, they watched three more riders come from the west, dismount and enter the saloon. Reaching the stairs that lead up to her shop, Nels hesitated. "How long will you stay tonight?"

"Only an hour or two. I have to be back here for

an appointment at nine tomorrow."

"Don't leave tonight until I come for you. Looks like there are a few at the saloon tonight. Three passengers came off the train late this afternoon when it came in and didn't leave with it. Until I find out why they are here, I want you to be careful, Sara. I don't want anything to happen to you. My sister-in-law would be very sad if I had to write that something had happened to you too. It was enough that her sister, my beloved Sophie, died so tragically."

"I'll lock the door from the inside when you leave with the padlock I used on the cabin door on the ship that I still have handy. I won't let anyone in. I'll pull the drape too so that I can't be seen in the window sitting at the machine working," shared Sara as she ascended the stairs to her shop. Nels waited and watched her close the door. When he heard the padlock close, he went back to the stable, unharnessed Stout and treated the horse to a small bucket of oats.

15 Alex

Nels set his cup on the sideboard near the basin, took his plate, empty now of the pancakes he'd made for breakfast, and placed it in the dish pan. Reaching for the kettle that sat at the back of the wood burning stove always ready with hot water, he poured enough to cover the dishes stacked in the basin, added a little chipped soap and scrubbed, placing the clean dishes on the drain board to dry. Silverware, mixing bowl and fry pan followed. Finished with his task, he grabbed the dish pan, walked to the back door of the two bedroom house he'd built when he and Sophie came to Goose, stepped out on the landing facing the south and scattered the sudsy water on the thin green spires peeking out of the heavy black soil. Returning to the kitchen and setting the pan back in its place, Nels checked the wood box and made sure that the coals in the stove were banked enough so the coals would smolder until evening when he and Sara returned. Grabbing his hat and jacket to brace against the strong wind sweeping down, he glanced to make sure the water kettle he'd refilled was in its place on the side of the stove, opened the door and made his way down the well rutted street to the Livery Stable.

Yesterday, the North Coast Limited had delivered enough lumber for a mahogany table and chairs along with the other birch, black walnut and cherry planking he'd ordered. He'd asked Rufus to see to its stacking in the Livery Stable, the only place lengths of planking could be stored with some protection against weather.

"Need a wagon?" offered Oscar as Nels entered the stable, hoping to have a reason to hook up his two draft horses and give them a workout they sorely needed. Harvest would come soon and there'd be offers a plenty to hire out the team. Oscar knew his horses needed conditioning before they were asked to walk a full day ahead of a plow, drag or sickle.

"No, just want to look at the lumber, see how long each of the planks is and then decide how I should cut what I need today so that I can take enough to the shop to start the table Mrs. Primrose ordered."

"You dealing with her?"

"Shouldn't I be?" asked Nels, curious to see what Oscar knew about the woman who'd come insisting on perfection, knowing little about carpentry and wood.

"Better make sure you please her," Oscar stated with firmness in his voice. "Lady is short on brains and long on tongue!"

"Sounds like you've had experience dealing with her."

"She rented a cart and horse to go to her quilting group that was meeting out at her brother's homestead two miles west of town. I asked her if she knew how to handle the reins. She said I should mind my own business and slapped the rein ends on Bart's rump. Bart took off on a gallop. The startled horse ran off with the cart and it careened down the rutted street with her yelling and screaming for help. Horse stopped short and she ended up in the water trough outside Lars'."

"Lars'? Oh, ja. You mean the trough in front of the Dry Goods Shop."

"Lars heard the commotion, came out and had all he could do not to laugh as the prim and proper Primrose hauled herself out of the tank. A tirade followed the likes of which shocked the men who came out of the saloon to see what all the commotion was about. None of them wanted anything to do with her and turned as quickly as they could, going back inside the saloon."

"Thanks for the warning. I'll keep that in mind, Oscar," and he headed back to where he had the lumber stacked. Coming near those stacks, Nels moved cautiously. Loud snoring came from the same area where the smell of new lumber wafted in the air and mingled with that of the drier wood stacked alongside his newly ordered supply. Nels gingerly walked to the chest high pile of lumber in front of him. He stuck his nose around the end cuts and was surprised to see a well-dressed younger man lying on top of his piled lumber, using the stack as a makeshift bed. His arm was his pillow. Clearing his throat loudly, Nels waited until the young man stirred and sat up. "At least you didn't carry any off," was Nels comment as he gestured to the woodpile.

"Sorry Sir. I came in on the last train, helped to unload the lumber and went to the rooming house to get a room. All the rooms were full. The rooming house lady told me that I could get a room today and I should come back this morning. The hotel rooms were full too. There was such a ruckus coming from the saloon by the doctor's office so I looked around and saw no other place that might have a room. I decided to come back here to the stable. Since I am not used to sleeping with horses, I chose the wood. I needed sleep. The smell of newly cut lumber comforts me so I came back here, lay down and promptly fell asleep." Looking around at the stacks, he continued, "I don't think I have harmed anything,"

"Looks like the stacks are just fine. How is your back? A little stiff from the hard surface?" teased Nels who somehow sensed that this young man could be trusted.

"I'm used to hard surfaces. Spend a fair amount of time cutting timber up north of here. Fellow I work for stops cutting in the spring. Place we cut is too wet right now. Buffers a slough and swamp. Too hard to get the logs out to any wagons or flowing water so they can be hauled to market. We won't begin cutting again until the stocked piles have been shipped by wagon or rail which will be later this summer when the boggy land dries. In camp, we sleep on planks just like these. I'm not used to ticking or the comfort it gives." Looking towards the animal stalls, he questioned, "You own the horses too?"

"Only two, my roan there and the Fjeld next to her."

"Want to sell the tan one? What did you call her, Fjeld?" asked the young man with hope etched all over his face.

"Fjeld is a Norse breed of horse, bred for heavy work and gentle riding. My father saw that she was shipped here. Can't do that. Stout was her favorite horse."

"Was? Her?" came quietly from the young man,

sensing he'd stirred memories wished to be forgotten.

"My wife Sophie. Died last year in a tragic accident."

"Sorry. Looks like it needs some riding and care. I'd be willing to do that if you'd trust me."

"Son, trust is not a problem. I can tell talking to you that you are a good person. My niece would not be happy."

"So it's her horse now, the niece? Would she sell it?"

"Don't think so. I'm Nels Jacobson," he offered as he extended his hand in greeting. My niece is Sara. I have the furniture shop next to Larson's Dry Goods. Sara has her dress shop above Lars'. Just before she died, my wife Sophie asked Sara to come and be her partner. Sara is quite the clothing designer."

Accepting the greeting the tall, blond, well-built young man stated, "Alex Alexanderson. Part of my family has a homestead not far from here north on the Goose."

"I know the area. Good farm land. Done any wood carving, Alex?"

"Spend my time carving when it's too wet or cold to cut trees."

"Interested in doing some carving for me while you wait to go back to logging? I've an order for a mahogany table and chairs. You see the wood there. The chairs are to have a leaf and vine carving in the wood portion at the top of the ladder back of the chair. I usually make Rossette chairs but Mrs. Primrose is insistent that the chair would not be stable unless there is a four inch carved board across. I haven't carved for so long I don't think I could do that well. I've talked to Sara about it. She is willing to draw the design. Said she'd do the carving too. She's never used carver's tools and I am afraid she'd cut herself. Nor does she have time."

"Sounds like something I could do. We could fancy up the table legs a little too, I would think."

"Why don't you see about that room at Marta's Boarding House, Alex. She should still be serving her pancakes too. I'd imagine you're hungry."

Grinning with the thought of the possibility of food, he said, "It's been a while since I've had a good meal."

"I'll take a look at the wood," answered Nels, pointing to the mahogany stack, "and see which pieces would be best for the table. Come back when you are settled. By that time I'll be ready to cut lengths and haul them to the shop."

Shaking hands again and thanking Nels for the offer of some work he'd enjoy, Alex took his satchel in his left hand and agreed to return. "I'll be back once I get settled in my room, eat something and change out of these clothes into more suitable woodworking clothes." As he walked towards the street, Nels heard him say, "Pancakes, wonder if they're as good as Cooks' back at camp? They'll be hard to turn down if they're offered."

16 Horses

Three horses with heavy packs situated precariously behind the saddles stood with their reins looped over the rail in front of Marta's Boarding House. "Room's probably not ready for me yet," mumbled Alex to himself. "Looks like those three men fixing to leave this morning are still here. I'll ask if I can change my clothes in a room somewhere and stash my carpet bag until my room's ready later on." His senses became aware of a young woman coming towards the Dry Goods Shop across the street, arms laden with small packages. Distracted by the sudden whinnying of one of the horses as she neared it tied to the shop's rail, she stumbled briefly on an uneven plank in the boardwalk. Small packages scattered, some at her feet and some near the horse's hooves. Dropping the handle of his carpet bag where he stood, Alex hurried across the street to help. "Careful. I'll get the ones under the horse." Grabbing the reins of the uneasy paint horse, Alex reached down and retrieved the three packages near the plank walk and tossed them up on the boarding. The fourth was wedged under the right front hoof. Coaxing gently in a soothing voice, Alex was able to move the animal enough to free the last parcel. In doing so, he reached down and grabbed the last sack just as the horse tried to rise on its front legs, bumping Alex with his front haunch when the horse reared. Alex went flying sideways and slammed into the boardwalk, landing in the rutted street that was muddy from last night's rainfall.

"Are you hurt?" spoke Sara from the boardwalk, looking down at the young person who came to help. She'd temporarily set all her small packages on the boardwalk. "Glad the reins were as tight as they were. Stopped him from doing more than just bumping you. I've lived with animals all my life. You can tell most often the temperament of horses by looking in their eyes. I worried when I saw where my finery packages had fallen. I don't like the eyes of this one," came from Sara as she pointed to the paint. "Here, let me help you get up," and she extended her arm to him for balance.

"You must be Sara," decided Alex.

"How do you know my name?"

"I chose to sleep on the lumber that's stored at the Livery Stable. Marta's rooming house was full. The ruckus coming from the saloon was so noisy and I needed a good night's sleep. Nels found me sleeping on his boards stacked in the livery. He spoke about you when I asked if the Fjeld horse, I think he called it, was his and for sale."

"I'll have to talk to him. We are from a small mountain berg in Norway. Strangers rarely came up the river to where we lived. He's too quick to share information with strangers." Trying to dismiss him and more conversation, she reached out her hand to help him.

Alex used the planking for support rather than dirtying her extended hand. He was very worried that his weight would pull her slight form into the muck as well. Alex righted himself and brushed off the mud as best he could. Checking the state of his only suit, he discovered a long tear from knee down on his left pant leg.

"You've torn you pants. You're bleeding too. Come with me. Let's see if you need stitches."

"You stitch wounds too?" asked Alex, with amazement in his voice as he followed Sara up the stairs and waited until she unlocked the trusty padlock she used on the ship. Remembering his satchel, he decided, "I'll be right back. I need to cross the street and retrieve my satchel that I set down when I saw your difficulties. It has all my belongings in it. Can't let it get away," and he gingerly made his way down the stairs again, favoring the left leg.

"If Uncle Nels trusts him, I should be able to," mumbled Sara as she set her small parcels down on top of a vanity that stood close to the sewing machine and found a swab cloth to clean the leg wound.

"Have trouble getting a room?" asked Nels when Alex returned more than two hours later.

"No, room was not the problem. Torn pants was."

"Torn pants? Whatever happened?" came from a surprised Nels.

"Horse reared and sent me stumbling into the planking in front of the Dry Goods Shop."

"Dry Goods Shop? It's on the opposite side of the street. You didn't stop at the saloon, did you? I don't tolerate drinking," declared Nels with a firmness in his voice.

"No, I rescued your niece," came from Alex with a smug smile on his face.

"Now wait a minute. You couldn't wait, could you! Need a woman that bad? The saloon has its contacts . . ." Nels didn't get a chance to finish his tirade. Alex stepped forward and held up his hand.

"Miss Sara had too many small packages in her hands as she made her way to her shop. She stumbled on an uneven plank when the paint that was hitched to the rail whinnied and distracted her. Some of the packages fell under the horse. Not wanting her to be stepped on, not knowing what the horse would do, I ran across and helped her. As I reached for the last small package under a front hoof, the paint tied to the rail reared as best it could. Its right haunch bumped me, sending me into the boardwalk and street muck. Tore my pants too."

"Wondered why you were favoring that left leg. You seem to have weathered your spill."

"Did. Got patched up by your niece. See." Alex rolled up his pant leg and displayed the bandage now wrapped around his calf. "Sews a pretty good flesh seam too. Bit my tongue to stifle the pain. Didn't want to show my weakness. Never can stand the sight of blood, especially when it's mine."

"Saw you walking over here with that little limp. How painful is it? Able to help load these mahogany planks into that wagon?"

"I think so. Will you hitch Stout – that the Fjeld's name – to the wagon? I'd like to see him work."

"Intend to. My roan wants nothing to do with pulling anything. I'm the only one he tolerates when he's saddled," said Nels as he moved to Stout's stall and began to harness the Fjeld.

"What can I do?" offered Alex. A blast from the west bound North Coast Limited's whistle vibrated through the air and Alex was unable to hear Nels' instructions. Waiting and watching the passengers step off the train, both men heard two women's high pitched voices ring out which caught their attentions.

The first to step off the platform onto the boardwalk whined, "Why did you bring me? My shoes aren't made for this kind of walking. The soles are too thin. I feel every uneven board and rock I step on, Juliet. Look at the muck. We'll never get our shoes clean if we have to cross the street." Looking around, she continued. "Oh, drat. The hotel is across the street. Whatever shall we do?" Alex eyed the small statured woman who looked like a barrel wearing a traveling suit nervously wringing her gloved hands. Both she and the suit were dusty from days on the train. Her hat, once full of feathers pointing upward to make her look taller, now sat insecurely on the back of her long black hair twisted into a bun.

"We're only spending a day here, Aunt Agnes. Just enough time to change our clothes, wash our hair and have a decent meal before we continue on our way to Billings."

"Have to be a good reason for my staying any longer," Alex heard the one called Aunt Agnes say. "This berg – is that what these people call this small village – is too small for my tastes." She stood still and gazed around. "I see a sign for a dentist across the street. Maybe he'll have time to look at that tooth that keeps paining you."

"You sure we won't be set upon by robbers? I don't see a sheriff's office, Aunt Agnes? As for the tooth, I'd rather not have him look at it. We have no idea how much experience he has. He may pull the wrong one," decided Juliet as she rubbed her left lower jaw.

"Alex. Alex. Stop your daydreaming and help me," ordered Nels. "If I'm going to pay you, I need your help."

"Sorry, sir. When we're out cutting wood, we see very few women. The shrill voices of those two make me realize how lucky I am not to have to listen to the likes of women like them every day."

The wagon had been hitched to Stout and the horse stood patiently waiting for the lumber to be loaded so he could pull. The short trip to the furniture shop demonstrated Stout's ability to react quickly to the slightest instructions, verbal as well as a gentle tug on the reins. "He's well trained. You do that?"

"Nay, I was already gone from the homestead when my father bought him. Sara and her grandfather, my father Jacob, trained him. The breed is mild tempered. An angel compared to some of the western horses I've seen around here."

"If the one that dumped me in the street was mine, I'd sell him. Like Sara said, you could tell in his eyes that he was skittish."

"Sara said, ha? Exactly how much time did you spend with my niece, Alex?" Alex had no time to answer because the two women from the train stepped in front him as he began to tie Stout to the rail in front of the furniture shop.

"Young man. When you have the lumber unloaded, please go to the train depot and get our trunks. They are on the platform. Bring them to the hotel and up to our room – Room 4. Hurry. We are so tired of being covered with dust." Finishing her instructions, the round barreled Agnes waddled back to the hotel.

"Of all the . . ."

"Alex, see with her eyes," offered Nels. "Look at

yourself. You are tying up a horse with a cart. She probably comes from a house full of servants. Won't hurt you to do your good deed for the day."

"On your time?"

"If I'm willing."

"Somehow I think I get the wrong end of this deal. Interested in bartering my services?" Alex smiled and waited for Nels' answer.

"What do you have in mind?"

"A little exercise for Stout and a chance for me to go to the river, use that pole I saw hanging on the stable wall, fish a little and see if I can catch supper for tonight."

"Fish? Haven't had fish since – can't remember last. Deal." Nels propped the heavy oak door to the furniture shop open and the two hauled the planking in and stacked it carefully on the south wall saw horses.

Finishing, Alex dusted himself off and removed the door prop. "Be back around four. You fine with that? Unless I can't get away from those two women," and he whistled a lilting tune as he quietly closed the door behind himself.

The street was a buzz of activity. Three other wagons came lumbering down the rutted street, two from the west and one from the east. Alex waited until they had passed. Untying Stout, he jumped up on the wagon seat and was surprised when the horse backed himself away from the rail without direction and headed for the train platform. Once there, Stout stopped at the rail. Throwing the reins over the post without securing them, Alex easily lifted each of the large trunks onto the wagon bed and re-boarded, grabbing the reins as he did so. Stout backed away once again but this time waited for instructions. A gentle tug to the right turned the horse and wagon around so both could cross over to the hotel. Stepping down and tying Stout to the rail,

Alex headed for the back of the wagon and the first trunk. Lifting it easily onto his shoulder, he dodged a woman who had a child in hand, set the trunk down long enough to open the hotel door, picked up the trunk again and walked to the stairs beside the clerk's counter. Seeing no one there, Alex began his ascent, reached the upper landing and looked for Room 4. Spying it just to the left, he stepped quietly to it, knocked gently and waited.

"What took you so long? Only one trunk? There were two," came from a harsh, high pitched voice of the one who'd opened the door Alex knew was called Agnes.

Alex didn't bother to answer her, just turned and headed back down the stairs. Stepping out to retrieve the last trunk, he jostled the hotel door open, crossed to where the stairs were and heard, "Young man. You can't go upstairs. You have no room here."

"I wish what you said was true – that I didn't need to go upstairs. That little woman in Room 4 is something else! She thought I was a delivery boy! Imagine that!"

The clerk grinned and then laughed out loud. "You're the one that got assigned the task. I wondered who they'd convinced. Told them we didn't have such people here, that they'd have to get their own trunks up to the room or leave them at the depot. The shorter one looked at me as if I had two heads, turned on her heels as best she could round as she is, and marched out the door. Where'd she find you?"

"Over at the Livery, getting ready to load Nels' lumber. I'm Alex Alexanderson. I'm going to do some wood carving for him."

"That Nels. He's so soft hearted," and no more was said since the voice from above disrupted the two.

"Young man. You're shirking your duty. Get that

trunk up here now. The bath water is getting cold."

"Wish I could dump it on your little head," whispered Alex as he hoisted the trunk on his shoulder and quickly ascended the stairs once again. Setting the trunk inside the door, Alex took one look at Agnes and declared, "That will be two dollars. A dollar for each trunk hauled," and held out his hand.

"Of all the . . ." Agnes stood a minute, contemplated what to do and finally went to her jacket lying on the bed. Turning her back to Alex so he could not see what she was doing, she removed two silver coins from an inside pocket. Turning back and walking forwards, she declared, "Here. Leave. It's not proper for a young man your age to be in a woman's room when she has no other woman companion present. Go. We'll need you in the morning an hour before the next train so we can have these trunks back at the station. Don't forget."

"You will need to find someone else, Ma'am. I work for one of the merchants here. I am not a livery boy for hire." A gasp was heard as Alex shut the door to Room 4, glad to be free of his responsibility and anxious to go fishing.

17
Celebrating

Banners strung across the fronts of buildings, some haphazardly and others secured with a 2 x 4 board, swayed in the gentle south wind. Late spring snows that had drifted in from the west made the heavy dark soil stick to the plows and tillers. This snow had delayed the start of spring planting. Good soil moisture from all the late snow and a few warm days had changed all that. Today, slight breeze bursts drifted across the green mass of the late planted grain that flanked Goose. Heads were already heavy. Summer heat and cool nights would mean a bumper crop, one sorely needed after last year's drought. The homesteaders, now called farmers, were glad for the respite, knowing their grain was already headed out but not ripe. Most had completed their first cutting of hay. The threat of grasshoppers swooping in and devastating the surrounding farmsteads always loomed in the minds of the farmers. The critters hadn't been pests for over seven years. Each hoped that this would not be a year to battle them.

With the main work done until the next hay cut, the calendar said it was time to celebrate. Covered wagons had been dusted off and supplied for a three day stay at Goose Crossing. Sara locked her shop door early, wanting to finish her own dress she intended to wear at the celebration.

The lace from her throat to bodice did not want to lay flat. Adjusting the dress form to her own measurements, she put the dress on the form so she could position the lace to the neck and collar. Lifting the dress off the form when she had her pins in place, Sara sat and delicately hand stitched the lace to the dress as she removed each pin that held the two fabrics together. Finishing, she hung the dress on the clothes tree Uncle Nels had made for her and went back to the window. A covered wagon came rumbling down the street headed towards the church where others had gathered. "Oh, my," uttered Sara as she put both hands to her mouth in prayer fashion. "I've never seen so many wagons gathered in one place. No wonder the mercantile and the dry goods store had so many extra boxes of supplies delivered." She watched the incoming wagon find a place in the second circle of wagons that was forming between the church and the river. Horses, mules and oxen milled together in a makeshift corral outside the wagon circles, content to eat the fresh grass and drink from the river. More children's voices filtered up to her as she watched and waited for Uncle Nels to come and join her for the first event of the weekend, the stew contest.

"Stew ready yet?" questioned Nels as he came to the back of his furniture store, filled today with the pungent smell of onions and fried bacon.

"Been at it just as dawn broke over in the east," Alex said. "Your little pot belly stove works well, Nels. Glad you offered to let me cook here. Easier than building a small fire out the back door. Hope the smell doesn't linger once I'm done. I'll see that the shop is aired properly and even cut a few of the log sections into planking so the smell of fresh cut wood lingers in here instead. That should sweeten the smell once again," decided Alex.

"How about a taste. Is it ready for a sample?"

"No. Don't have the potatoes in yet. Just put the carrots in. Cooked much?" asked Alex, waiting for what he thought the answer would be.

"Part of the reason I married. Never had to cook. Never learned. Can make a good soup if I have to. Who can't? You start by browning meat and add vegetables."

Alex smiled. "Camp Shack Stew the way Cook

makes it starts with squirrels. I shot eight, skinned and deboned them. Cut the meat into bite size pieces." Nels came to look when Alex opened the lid of a sizable flat frying pan with tall sides that could serve as a cooking pot.

"Smells like more than squirrel in there."

"Ja, as you say," voiced Alex with a wide grin. "Bacon's first. That's what you smelled when you first came in, right?"

"Made me hungry even if I've had my ration of oatmeal this morning."

"Need to fry the bacon for flavor but also for grease to lightly brown the squirrel. Squirrel doesn't have much grease of its own and burns more than fries if you're not careful."

Looking in the pan, Nels asked, "Where'd you get the corn kernels and the beans? Looks like limas to me."

"Before I left camp, Cook packed what he hoped was a 'Survivor Kit' for me. Two packages of dried fixings for stew and two packages of corn bread mix. Cook always uses lima beans. They're a bigger bean and fill up the kettle and the stomach faster. Made more volume to fill the hungry wood cutters he fed. The corn kernels you see in the base soften and thicken the stew."

"Corn bread? What's that? Any different from other bread?"

"With your Norse upbringing, cooking was woman's work. Right? You probably never had to cook much, especially out in the open – rely on flat rocks at the side of a fire for your oven. Corn bread is made from dried corn kernels, mashed as close to flour as possible. I add water to the mash to make a dough. Spoonsful of dough are dropped on cleaned, flat rocks beside the fire and baked until done. I wiped off the surface of your pot belly stove here before I started. I'll use the top and bake some bread just before it's time to take the stew out for judging." Alex stirred the stew and added three cut up tomatoes he'd bought at the mercantile. Paid dearly for them too.

"What time is judging?"

"Four thirty this afternoon, about an hour from now. Awards follow and then people can pay their ten cents for a sample. Money goes to the town council who is looking to buy some kind of firefighting rig."

"How big a sample do you give? How many are competing?" came from the frugal Nels. He was generous in some ways but very tight with his penger.

"Have no idea. When I walked earlier to get tomatoes, I saw four who were tending their fires and pots. Haven't been out to see if more have joined them. I understand from the rules posted at the bank that we register at the tables set up in front of Dr. Harem's office. We bring our stew pots to the serving tables that are set up near there too."

"Who are the judges?"

"I couldn't tell you. Even if I knew their names, I still wouldn't know much. Haven't been here long enough to be acquainted with names and faces."

"Did you take your carvings that you did of the settlers over to Pearson's Apothecary yesterday for display and judging? Hope you took the old man sitting on the stump with his cane pole in his hand and the fish dangling at the other end of the string that is his fishing line."

"Took that one and another you haven't seen, I believe."

"What one's that?" came from Nels as he moved closer to the back door where Alex now positioned himself on one of Nels' Rossetti chairs. As Alex talked, he sat carving a leaf design into the four inch walnut

board that spanned another of Mrs. Primrose's ordered chairs.
"My favorite, the lumberman that I am. A woodcutter stands with axe in hand, ready to make the last chip on the right side of a standing tree before it falls to the ground."
"You carved the tree too?"
"No, a portion of one that stands taller than the woodcutter. Have to be careful when I move the woodcut. The axe comes loose from his hand and the handle could break easily. The handle's that finely carved."
"Since you're not going to feed me a sample, I'll go take a look at the opposition," uttered Nels. "If you're going to hand out samples, you need all you have in that pan I'd guess. Next time you decide to make stew, I'll shoot the squirrels and clean them. Give you some penger for the fixings too. Don't wait too long. Even if the weather is changing, becoming warm. We still . . ." and their conversation was disrupted by the shrill voice of the one client Nels was sorry he'd promised furniture.
"Mr. Jacobson, are you here? It's seems so dark when you come out of the sun into this shop. My, what smells so good? You a cook too? Is that a stew I smell? Are my chairs finished?" Questions came nonstop from Mrs. Primrose as she made her way to the back of the shop. "You're the carver?" tumbled out of her mouth amid coughs and gasps, recognizing Alex as the person who'd first delivered the trunks off the train. She inhaled the fragrance of stew mixed with the smell of wood. "You can cook too?"
"He is both the carver and the cook, Mrs. Primrose, and a good one at that. I know the stew smells good. Look at the three chairs he's finished for me. The detail is so finely carved that you can see the

veins on the leaves," responded Nels.

Walking to the three chairs, her rotund body spilled over the side of the seat of one she chose to sit on while she closely examined the detail on another. "You are right. The veins are very visible. Fine work, young man. When will the six be done? Since Juliet and I have decided to stay here in Goose, we will be looking for a more permanent place than the hotel. The riffraff that come in on the train and lodge there for a day or two are not to our genteel upbringing. We are nurses. In fact, Juliet has midwife training. Dr. Harem is interested in employing the two of us, having us help out when he is away from Goose making house calls at the farms or are they homesteads? I get confused these days."

Rattle on she did – like rain pouring off a roof! Nels was glad to hear that the two women would be kept busy. He knew Sara kept her distance from this woman as much as possible, finding Primrose a gossip, a shrew and a nosy person with more time on her hands than sense in her head. Nels couldn't wait to relay the information to his niece. Sara wouldn't have to be so cautious about being seen sewing by the window's natural light that fronted the street across from the hotel. Mrs. Primrose would have her nose in other people's goings on. Nels had made sure to caution Sara about Room 4 in the hotel across the street. When Sara gazed out her window and directly across the street, she looked into the opposite upstairs window of Room 4 where Mrs. Primrose and Juliet roomed since coming in on the train.

"You wool-gathering, Mr. Jacobson. I asked you a question. When will the chairs be done?"

"Alex, what do you think?" Nels decided not to directly answer the question, rather defer it to Alex.

"I'd think early next week. With the 4th of July

celebration this weekend, I am not sure how much carving I'll get done."

"You don't demand specific hours from him, Mr. Jacobson?" she questioned with amazement in her voice.

"No, we operate under a handshake and an understanding, a common method of agreement for people who settled here. Paper is not always at hand. Some here aren't able to write or read for that matter. A simple handshake can tell a lot about a person." Nels stopped short, realizing he'd been drawn in to one of Mrs. Primrose's means of gathering information. "My judgment hasn't failed me yet. Alex is a fine young man. I'm so glad he agreed to carve for me." Nels continued to talk as he extended his hand to the seated woman, offering to help her up and on her way. "Thank you for stopping. I will leave a message with Carl, the hotel clerk, when the chairs are ready."

"I'll be waiting. Don't take too long, young man," came over the shoulder from the huffing woman as she reached the street entrance.

Nels followed her to the entrance and looked down the street to the front of the saloon. Chairs sat on each side of the saloon doors offering a place for the locals to gather and talk. Tables for the stew judging stood ready but empty near Dr. Harem's office, waiting for the competition to begin. Spotting a total of nine small fires with pots hanging over them, Nels walked back to Alex and found him grinning from ear to ear. "When you compared her to a barrel, you were right. Glad to hear she's found something to keep her busy. Wonder if Doc will be out of town more when he finds out what a shrew she is? Can't imagine spending one hour with her, much less a full day!"

"Any way I can help you get those chairs done sooner so she stops coming by?" offered Nels in a harsh voice.

"Never seen you so upset, Nels."

"Having you grinning like you were when I came back didn't help my temperament. Sorry. Most times I can ignore a person like that and not be so critical. Maybe I need to get out of town too and clear the cobwebs that form when one is in one place too long. See you later. I'm going to tell Sara the news. Don't feel chained to the chairs. She'll get them when we have them done. I didn't give her a definite date and neither did you." Grabbing his hat, he made his way to Sara's dress shop, hoping she was not inundated with clients and he could sit a while with her and pass time.

18 Events

Eric opened the door of his blacksmith shop, took off his leather apron and hung it on its peg by the side of the door. Heading to wash at the water trough next to the windmill, he spotted Nels coming down the street and went to meet him. "Nels, Alex have his stew ready for the contest?"

"How'd you know he's making stew, Eric?"

"Came to see if I had a large pot for sale. Didn't have one. The covered wagons have wiped me out. Asked Alex what he needed so large a pot for and he told me about his stew."

"If the smell's any indication, it'll be good. Why you cleaning up so soon? It looks like you still have work to do," came from Nels as he looked down the street at the pole lying in front of the water tower.

"You're right. I do have more work to do. Just

came out to take a layer of black soot off my hands. Jonas will be here shortly and we will grease the pole and set it in the hole for the contest."

"Hope we won't have so many slivers to deal with this year as we did last."

"Alex did as good a job as he could with his scraping knife" was Eric's answer. "The wood is solid and green. That should help too. You're lucky that young man decided to sleep on your lumber in the livery stable when he came out of the logging camp that night. Think he'll stay around and not go back come fall when the sloughs dry?"

"Not sure, Eric. He's making good money working for me and it isn't the hard work that logging is. Only time will tell. I see Jonas coming. I'm going to Sara's to wait upstairs until it's time to taste the stews. When the pots are in line for tasting, we'll come down and enjoy the festivities." Walking to the dress shop entrance, he opened the door and called, "Sara. Sara shall I come up or are you ready?"

"Come up for just a minute, Uncle Nels. I'm not quite ready." Nels entered the shop, walked to the window and looked down on the street below.

Sara pointed to the clothes tree and said, "Like my new dress?"

"Oh, Sara, you've outdone yourself. The ladies will be jealous when they see you wearing it tomorrow."

"The pattern is made from one of the magazines that Rufus found on the train." She took one look to see that her hat was placed properly on her head and opened the door. "I'm ready." Taking the padlock and key in hand, she turned the sign on its peg to read CLOSED, shut the door behind them and padlocked the hinge, slipping the key into her little bag on her wrist. Lifting her skirt so she wouldn't stumble, she bounced down the stair a little less than ladylike, anxious to be out and about. "Uncle Nels, I've never seen so many people in Goose."

"You've not been here for any celebrations, Sara."

"Do the covered wagon people come to all the celebrations?"

"Depends on the time of year. Goose Crossing has a Spring Fling. Most come then to buy or barter for seed for the gardens and fields. I see more wagons circled today to celebrate the 4th of July than we've had before. More people are coming west to settle. The Fall Harvest Ball in October will bring those who want to really dress up and dance. Sophie was always so busy then making the fancy dresses. You will be too, I'm sure. Usually those who come for the Harvest Ball and for the Christmas Market stay either at Marta's or at the hotel. Sleeping in the covered wagon that time of year might be too cold for most who are not used to doing so."

Settling themselves on a bench in front of Doctor Harem's office, Sara took the small flyer she'd been given to post in her shop and looked at the scheduled events. "The only activity tonight is this stew contest?"

"It used to be tomorrow, Saturday at noon. When the town council decided to have a pig roast as a fund raiser, the stew contest was moved to the night before."

"Who's the speaker tomorrow? Do you know, Uncle Nels?"

"Teddy Roosevelt will be here. He'll arrive on the west bound North Coast Limited on his way to his ranch in the western part of the Dakotas."

"I heard one of the women talking about him. He's campaigning to save the Badlands, right? How will I know who he is, Uncle Nels?"

"You can't miss him in a crowd. He always

wears a hat, has a mustache, is round in body like Mrs. Primrose but has skinny legs. And, he wears spectacles."

"Here comes Alex with his pan of stew."

"Wait here, Sara. I'll see if he needs any help."

Nels had no more than gotten up and a lady sat down by Sara. "I hope I'm not interrupting anything. I saw you sitting by Nels Jacobson. You must be Sara, Sophie's niece that she was so anxious to have come. I'm so sorry to hear about her passing. She was a good woman."

"Had she promised to make something for you? I don't think I've missed an order."

"No. My name is Mrs. Olson. Please call me Faith. I am wondering if you have time for a fitting sometime before we leave on Sunday afternoon. We come for the Harvest Ball and I'd like a new dress for it."

"Are you an early morning person? We could meet at the shop at 8 AM if that would be suitable, Mrs. Olson."

"It's Faith, dear," came from the lady with a sweet voice. "Eight is just fine. I will see you then," and she stood and walked towards the hotel.

"Who was that?" asked Nels as he and Alex came to sit on the same bench with Sara. "I don't remember seeing her in Goose before."

"One of Aunt Sophie's former customers. She wants me to make her a dress for the Harvest Ball. I'm to meet her in the shop at eight in the morning."

"Sara, I've spoken to Nels," said Alex, "and he's given me permission." Sara's eyes flew towards Nels, wondering what he'd promised. "There's a wheelbarrow race tomorrow. I'd like you to ride in my wheelbarrow. Would you do that?"

"Will there be others my age in other barrows?"

"All the kids line up for the foot races, the sack races and the high jump. Few climb the greasy pole."

"You didn't answer my question, Alex. Are there others our ages that participate in the wheelbarrow race?"

"Truth is I wanted to ask you before Henry does. Nels tells me he's won the race the last four years. I'd like to challenge him. You willing?"

"Will the barrow ruin my new dress that I've worked so hard to have done?"

"We have a blanket at the house that you can put in the base of the barrow. It will protect your dress. I'll help you get seated, if you want," offered Uncle Nels.

"And when the race is over, how do I get out of the barrow?" came from the always practical Sara.

"I'll tip it up on its front and give you a hand out."

"Sounds better to me than what happened to Marie last year. Henry got to the finish line and dumped her out. It was a funny site to see her scramble for dignity," added Nels.

"Wish she were not married and still here. I'd love to challenge her," quipped Sara with an edge in her voice.

"I won't sign us up until late tomorrow so we won't stir a fuss. You'll have to have an answer for Henry if he comes asking, Sara. I'll leave that up to you. Think I'd better check on my stew. Looks like the judging is done. I think you'd better get in line if you're doing any tasting." What he said was true. People were moving down the street from all directions towards the judging table and the stew samples.

"Won't be enough for all these people to sample. Some of the pots I saw were pretty small, Sara. Marta stopped me earlier today and invited us to supper at her boarding house. I accepted, hoping that would be fine with you," said Nels. "Let's sample Alex's stew and head to her house and out of this crowd that's forming."

"Good. You know I don't like crowds. Alex is on the far end. Could we walk by all of them? I'd like to see what each pot looks like." Nels took Sara's hand, linked it to his elbow and walked with her towards the tables. None of the participants noticed that they were not sampling. Each was too busy ladling samples into small cups. Sara turned away from one sample. The smell of garlic permeated the air so strong that it caused her to sneeze. Few were sampling that pot. Alex stood waiting for them with cups he'd set aside for them. "Almost gone, Alex?"

"I'm surprised too. Should have made more. Would have if I'd known that the wagon drivers would come to town. I like being around people. I miss that when I'm with the logging crew. Here," and he reached under his frying pan lid. "I've saved two samples for you" and he handed over two of the cups still very warm to the touch.

"I'll see you at Marta's after I'm done here. Hope she's not making stew too. I've had enough of that smell for a while," said the grinning Alex. "Keep the spoons. I've carved one for each of you to have."

Looking at the handle of hers, Sara saw SJ carved in a leaf. Nels had NJ carved in the same leaf design. Moving away from the table, Nels said, "He must have done this carving at night. First I've seen these, Sara. How is the stew?"

"Good, Uncle Nels. Can't tell its squirrel. Tastes more like beef." When both were finished with their sample, Sara took the two spoons and wrapped them in a small cloth she found in her bag and slipped the purse back on her wrist. Both went to compliment Alex and found his spot empty. A lettered sign lay on the table where he'd been and said, 'Sold Out'."

As they walked, the two had to dodge around a platform in their way being constructed on the boardwalk. "What is being built now, Uncle Nels?" Sara questioned as they walked beyond the Doctor's office.

"Lucas heard about a minstrel show group that would be traveling on the Limited going west to perform in Moorhead tomorrow night. He asked them to stop over here and perform for us. Once we're done eating supper at Marta's, we'll come back here and see the show."

"Minstrel. I don't know that word."

"Sorry, I forget, Sara. A minstrel show can be black people playing the banjo, singing songs and dancing or it can be white people who blacken their faces. The troupe usually ends with a short, funny play."

"How do we get tickets?"

"Because it'll be outside here, Lucas will have fellows help him pass the hat and ask people to donate rather than sell tickets. Not the best way to collect funds but it works in a pinch." Reaching for the door handle to Marta's, he was surprised when it opened.

"Oh, you're here. I was just going to look and see how the stew sampling was going. Sara," said Marta as she reached to give her a hug. "So glad you came. We've not had a chance to talk much. Come to the kitchen. I've set a special table for the four of us. Alex is coming?"

"He's sold out so I'm sure he's back at the furniture store cleaning up his mess. Should be here shortly," said Nels. "Doesn't smell like stew, Marta."

"It's my mama's famous spaghetti sauce. I don't make it very often. Takes all day to make just the sauce. I make the noodles too."

"Sounds like a lot of work, Marta," decided Sara, used to making meals fast after she got home from the shop.

"It is. We'll see how you like it. I've placed dish towels by your plates. Tie them around your neck like a bib when you sit down. Don't want to spoil a pretty dress or shirt. The sauce is hard to wash out unless you can use lye for a bleach." That said, she turned and began filling the bowls headed for the dining room and her guests.

"How about I carry and you dish," offered Sara standing and moving to the stove.

"Thank you, Sara, for offering. Don't spill on yourself." The two worked in tandem, one dished and the other carried. Placing smaller bowls on the table she'd set for four, Marta went back to the dining room to check on her guests and found Alex seated there. She walked to him and quietly invited, "Alex, come to the kitchen I have a surprise for you." She turned and he rose and followed her.

Sara was the first to ask, "Did you win?"

"Second place. One of the judges did not like the idea that I'd used squirrel meat, I guess. When they announced the winner, those standing around booed! Most thought I should have won. This smells good, Marta. Thanks for asking me to come."

"Nels, will you pray?" Heads bowed and Nels offered a blessing for food, friends and family and all joined with an "Amen.

"Eat all you want but save room for dessert. I've made German chocolate cake. Jon finally got a shipment of coconut at the mercantile. I've had it on order for over a year, I'd swear."

Conversation flowed easily among the four about ripening grain, the threat of a fire from the lack of rain, the need for a fire wagon, the excitement to see the minstrel show, and the concern centered around more strangers in Goose more often.

The meal and dessert finished, Marta offered her guests a chance to relax in her parlor when she put the meal away. Nels and Alex graciously accepted her offering. Sara hung back and began cleaning off the table. "No need for you to help me, Sara. I'm used to doing this task alone."

"I know. Mor always said 'More hands make the task lighter'. This gives us a chance to visit too."

"Miss your mother and your family, do you?"

"Sometimes at night I do but I'm too busy, Marta, to even think about them much. Aunt Sophie was right in asking me to come. The shop does need two people most of the time. If I stay, I'll need to find someone to help me."

"You need a young man in your life, Sara. You work too hard for a young person like you. Interested in anyone here?"

"Haven't had much time to think about it. Henry's been a gentleman pest, if there is such a thing."

"What do you mean by that, Sara?"

"He'll pick flowers and leave them at the shop entrance with a note. Seems to be right there when a door needs opening, just like a little puppy dog wanting attention. Small things like that . . ." Marta kept silent, wanting her to talk more if she needed to. "He has no ambitions. He's the oldest so he gets daddy's barber shop business. Does he even know how to cut hair?"

"You're right, Sara. I don't think God put Henry on this earth to be your life mate. There'll come another. Be patient. That's the last of the mess cleaned up. It's soon time for the show. We better get out there and find a place to sit."

"Thank you for listening, Marta." A tear slowly drifted down her cheek as she hugged the lady she classified as a true friend.

As the two opened the door to the parlor and entered the room, Nels stood. "Alex is outside finding us seats. Are you ready for the show?"

"I'm ready for a good laugh, Nels. It's been a while since I've experienced a real belly rumbler! Let's see if we can find Alex."

Alex had moved a bench he'd found down the street over in front of Doctor Harem's, making a second row in front of the stage that had been built for the troupe. Other men were doing the same for their families. The bench was just long enough so all four could sit comfortably and wait. The four sat together talking and waiting for the minstrel show to begin.

19 Shows

The gathered audience quieted when three couples walked up the steps of the make-shift stage. Each person in some way was dressed in red, white and blue in honor of Independence Day. Two men came behind and sat to the left of the stage and began strumming banjos. The program started with the group singing "In the Good Old Summertime" in perfect harmony. Quickly the men took their partners and the banjos strummed "After the Ball" as the couples danced the waltz. To liven up the program, the group taught the audience the chorus of a new song called "Ta-ra-ra-Boom-de-ay." Next, the three couples exchanged partners and danced a new dance called the two-step to the delight of the audience. The final song before the group changed costumes was "The Girl I Left Behind Me" in honor of those serving in the war. When the troop went to change clothes, the banjo players came up on stage and strummed two songs: "Li'l Liza Jane" and "Turkey in the Straw." Alex and Sara joined other audience members and clapped and sang along. Lucas had arranged for the group to sing spirituals instead of doing a slapstick plantation skit. Dressed in black, the group of six joined the banjos on stage and sang "Nobody Knows the Trouble I've Seen" and "Balm in Gilead" in perfect harmony. The group finished their show with "This Ol' Time Religion."

When the crowd began to leave after the last song, Sara and Nels said goodbye to Marta and Alex and walked back home with a lightness in their step. "Do entertainers like this group come often?" asked Sara.

"Not often enough, I'm afraid. We don't have a place with a stage besides the small one in the saloon. We don't have an empty building that is big enough to hold a lot of people. Deacon and the bishop won't let us use the church." Reaching the door, Nels offered, "If you need to be at the shop early in the morning to meet that Olson woman, don't take the time to start tomorrow's breakfast for us. It is late already. I think we've fresh bread in the bread keeper. A slice of that with butter and jelly will do fine."

Sara climbed the steps leading to her bedroom and turned midway, "Thanks for your concern for me, Uncle Nels, and for asking me to come here. Goose is feeling more like home every day I'm here" and she continued up the stairs.

Morning came too early for Sara. The sun shining in her window facing east woke her from her dream of the mountains back home. She was being chased down the mountain by a mountain goat. "What brought back that memory, I wonder?" mumbled Sara as she climbed out from under her comforter, washed and dressed quickly. She put one of her every-day dresses on, knowing she was going to change into the new dress that hung in her shop that she'd just finished for herself once she'd met with Mrs. Olson. Taking her uncle's suggestion when she got downstairs, she cut a slice of bread, buttered it and generously spread jelly on top. Putting her shawl and hat on, she quietly opened the door into the sunshine and enjoyed her breakfast as she walked. Reaching the shop ahead of Mrs. Olson, she changed her mind and switched into her new dress. Next, she found a measuring tape, a pencil and paper to write on. Hearing footsteps on the stairs, she went to the door and opened it. "Mrs. Olson, I'm glad you've come. Come in and sit a minute. Is that a pattern you have in your hand?"

"Faith, girl. I feel younger when people call me by my first name. Yes, it is. I hope it is not too risqué a dress for this area. It's a picture of a dress I found in the **New Yorker** magazine. Can you copy it and make it for me?"

Sara took the picture in hand, studied it a bit and asked, "What are your intentions for the fluff I see around the neck area, Faith?"

"I suppose it could be fur but I think I'd rather have some fluffy lace instead. Do you have anything suitable available or do I need to go downstairs and see what is in the mercantile?"

"I have more lace in the shop up here then they have downstairs. Aunt Sophie sent for a generous supply, knowing I was coming. Let's see what I have first. We have time so Mrs. Larson can order if I don't have anything suitable." Sara went to her stash of boxes that she knew contained lace and opened three until she found the one she was looking for. "This might work. What do you think, Mrs. Olson?" Seeing her frown, Sara remembered and quickly added. "Sorry, Faith."

"This will work just fine if you bunch it up as much as you can to make it fluffy."

"The dress will be ready for you when you come for the ball. Come see me as early as you can when you get here so I can check the fit and be sure it is just right for you."

"The dress you are wearing is absolutely stunning. I wish I were closer and I'd have you sew more for me. I've yet to find a good seamstress in Georgetown. I usually order from **Sears Roebuck** and hope it fits."

"Where is Georgetown, Faith? Far from here?"

"Not so far if you were a bird." Faith smiled and continued. "Georgetown is northwest of here. You either need to take the train to Moorhead or a horse or something pulled by one. At Moorhead, you follow an old oxcart trail that the traders and trappers used, now a gravel road. Georgetown was one of the first Hudson Bay Company trading posts in the area. Mr. Olson is one of the Bonanza farmers in that area. We own land on the opposite side of the Red River that runs north to Winnipeg. Thank you for your help in making my dress. Now I'll have something to look forward to when we next come to Goose Crossing. My husband is waiting. I must go. You do your Aunt Sophie proud, dear."

Faith gathered her shawl and small silver purse and gently closed the door behind herself.

Sara took the material Faith had left, put the lace she'd found with it along with the measurements and placed the stack on a shelf she'd had Uncle Nels put on the wall for just this purpose. The fitting had gone much smoother than she thought it would. The room was tidy for a sewing room. The floor was swept and spools of thread she'd used yesterday were back in their boxes. Walking to the wall shelf, she looked at her stack of orders and decided not to start on the one next in line. She was about to sit at the window seat when she heard "Sara child, are you up there?"

Recognizing Marta's voice, she answered, "I am. Want me to come down?"

"No, I'll climb." Reaching the landing at the top, Marta paused a moment and came into the shop. "You need to consider moving somewhere where there aren't any stairs. We old ladies struggle to climb them."

"What a pleasant surprise. First, you're not an old lady. Second, I don't think there's another place in Goose to rent. What are you doing out and about so early in the day?"

"Told the boarders they'd have to fend for themselves today. Church always does a barbeque at noon. The hotel makes sandwiches and sells them outside from a table Carl sets up in front their building. The boarders won't starve if I don't cook for them one day." Marta paused a bit and gave Sara a motherly look. "You seem nervous. Mrs. Olson's fitting not go well?"

"No. She's such a nice lady. I've another problem I'm not sure I've solved in the right way. Alex has asked me to be in the wheelbarrow race with him. I'm not sure it is proper for me to do that."

"Worried what might happen to that gorgeous

new dress?"
"No, more what might happen to my dignity."
"Trust him, Sara. He'll see that you are not put in an embarrassing situation. Asked you to take a boat ride with him yet?"
"No," Sara answered with hesitancy in her voice.
"He will. Come, take your parasol. Let's go down and watch the young folk race."
Opening the door that led to the street, Sara was amazed at the number of young people gathered around. "Before we build a dance hall or a theater, we need a school, Marta."
"Only about half of these children are locals. The rest are with the covered wagons."
"Doesn't matter where they're from. School is important. I'll ask Uncle Nels to talk to the council the next time it meets. I know a fire engine is important. So is a school." Three bells ringing at once stopped her. "What are all the bells ringing for Marta?"
"The church bells ring when the barbeque is ready. The west bound train arrived with Teddy Roosevelt just before I came up to see you. The foot races will start when all the commotion settles down. Let's see if we can find a place to sit next to the stage where Roosevelt will speak." Sara followed closely, letting Marta make a path for them through the people gathering in front of the hotel. Marta covered her mouth with a handkerchief as she turned and spoke in a whisper to Sara. "That's him coming to the stage now. He comes through often on his way to his ranch. He loves to hunt, work the cattle on the ranch and explore the Badlands."
The people moved forward from all directions and began to crowd the stage where Roosevelt was seated. He spoke only a short time, aware that the train needed to stay on schedule. "My friends, we need

to pass laws to protect the Badlands from overgrazing and overhunting. I move my herd systematically to allow regrowth, giving the land a chance to recover from the grazing. Pronghorn and mountain goats roam at will today but won't continue to do so if a limit isn't set dictating how many one person can shoot each season." The train whistle gave a short toot. "I need to board the train so it can stay on schedule west. Help me in any way you can to preserve and protect the beauty and serenity of the Badlands I've learned to love so much." Descending the makeshift stairs, he waddled towards the train platform and boarded just as the last warning whistle blew.

Too nervous to eat and worried about the upcoming race, Sara sent Nels and Marta over to the church without her. A barbeque sandwich did not sound good. She returned to her shop, sat on the chair by the window and waited for Alex to come and get her for the wheelbarrow race. Looking out, she saw five couples of varying ages, each gathered around a barrow. Sticking her head out the open window, Sara saw Alex come out of Eric's blacksmith shop. He wheeled a small but deep barrow that looked made to fit her behind and not at all like the other wheelbarrows the other contestants had. "That's a wheelbarrow? They can be that small?" uttered Sara as she continued to look out. Seeing Alex look up at her window, she signaled that she would come down and bring along the blanket Nels had found for her. When she got downstairs and near Alex, she heard two of the participants arguing with him.

"Nowhere in the rules is a size of the wheelbarrow mentioned. I had this one made to haul my carving scraps to the kindling pile," Alex said in defense of the strange size.

Sara stood aside and waited for the two unhappy

challengers to leave. Alex smiled at her but said nothing as he took the blanket and positioned it so her dress would be protected. Numbers were called for positions in the race. Alex and Sara were right in the middle of the nine racers. Sara looked at the competition and was glad that Henry was not one of the participants.

Alex spoke to her in a low voice so the others could not hear. "Sara, expect some pushing and shoving. Keep your hands protected so they don't get pinched or cut from the other barrows. I had this one made on an angle so that should not happen but I want you to be careful."

Flushed from the excitement of the race and the uncertainty of it all, she asked, "When do I get in?"

"The first time Rufus blows his whistle. When that happens, we have about five minutes to get ready for the second whistle. Are you still willing?" A slight nod was her response. "Trust me, Sara. I would not have you hurt for the world."

The first whistle blew and the women contestants settled in the wheelbarrows. A crowd gathered to cheer for their favorite. Out to the left she saw Marta and Uncle Nels standing watching. The second whistle blew and they were off. Sara slouched down into the belly of the barrow, placing her hands on her lap. One bump forced her forward and she grabbed onto the sides, glad that the front wheel was high enough off the ground so her shoes didn't hit the dirt and flip her out. Reaching the turn-around post, Alex wasted little time and was out ahead of the others who had larger barrows needing a bigger space to turn. Alex ran as fast as he could over the rough ground and watched Sara bounce as he hit ruts. Finishing first, he carefully stopped and gave Sara a hand so she could get out on her feet. Marta bombarded her with a hug and praise for her bravery. Uncle Nels patted Alex on his shoulder and gave Sara a big hug too. Others came forward and congratulated them. Eric was the last to come. "Good engineering, Alex. You were right. The barrel size was the key. You turned much faster than the rest. I've already got two more orders for barrows like yours." Alex and Sara's names were called and Lucas handed them each a five dollar gold piece. Sara turned to Alex and offered her piece to him, "You earned this, not me. All I did was sit."

"Oh, no. This was a team effort. I needed someone your slight size to fit in the barrow and willing to risk getting dirty if we were bumped."

Marta interrupted the two. "Come to the house. We need to celebrate the win. I've made another German chocolate cake. Made lemonade too."

Alex looked at Sara with a sheepish grin on his face. "Want to ride, Sara? I have to get this back to the boarding house so it doesn't get swiped."

"Why not!" muttered the girl, no longer fearing what people might say about her and climbed in once again.

20 Harvest

The meandering river came from the east and flowed west and north of Goose Crossing. It was deep enough in its center to allow hulled, flat bottomed boats to easily come and go. The farmers who'd settled up and down the river used this means to bring fresh produce to the communities that had formed along its route. Goose was one of those many small bergs formed close to the river as the families came in and settled. Milk, cream, freshly made butter, breads, eggs, broom bases made from the shafts of grain, sometimes items of knit clothing – whatever the acreage produced and was not needed – came to market on Saturdays.

Alex was content carving for Nels and running a delivery wagon transporting the shipments that came in on the train. Both kept him very busy so he did not return to the logging camps. Nels was extremely pleased with this decision and glad to have the excellent carver in his employ. He felt himself becoming agitated from lack of work, unused to idle time on his hands. Having a capable young man like Alex meant he could leave him in charge when he was gone, so Nels sought another way to be busy during the harvest season when furniture sales were slow. In late July through September, the locals were too engrossed in their dealing with gardens and crops to worry about more furniture. Only time an order came in was if a chair broke and couldn't be repaired.

Spending his idle time reading the magazines that train travelers left behind, Nels became intrigued with an advertisement, talked to the blacksmith and the two ordered the piece of equipment. Daily they waited for the train to arrive with their new adventure. Eric Hammer, Goose's blacksmith, and Nels agreed on a

partnership. Nels' portion was to make sure that the bindings and the wood structure of the McCormick Reaper the two purchased were in working order. Eric was responsible for the Reaper's metal parts, including keeping the sickle sharpened. Any money made would be split 70 – 30. 70% going to Nels who had invested that much money in the reaper and was to use Stout as the horsepower with himself as the operator. Eric was to get 30% for his investment and provide the upkeep needed on the metal.

About supper time on a hot summer day two weeks after they thought the equipment would be delivered, the Limited arrived late due to boiler problems at the St. Cloud stop south and east of Goose. The train's departure was further delayed by the unloading of the McCormick Reaper Nels ordered from the International Harvester Company.

Sitting in an open space beside Goose's water tower, the new equipment piece drew the townspeople, curious to see what the contraption was. Wanting to demonstrate the Reaper's capabilities, Nels asked permission from Harmen Olson whose farm land bordered the railroad track. "Harmen, your winter wheat is about a week away from harvest, I'd guess. Would you let me swath a short winnow to demonstrate the Reaper's capabilities?"

"Sure, I'm curious too. What'd you say it does, shucks grain into bundles?" boomed his strong bass voice. Harmen was one of the well-respected locals now leasing land from the railroad company and raising grain on it.

"Ties those bundles too so they are ready to put into shocks. You'll see." Nels carefully hitched Stout to the Reaper and set out to cross the tracks at the far end of the field. Positioning Stout and the reaper at the edge of the row, Nels made sure that the blade was in place and the binder loaded correctly with twine. Stepping carefully, he boarded the seat provided on the Reaper. A soft tap with the reins and Stout moved forward with a slow capable trot. Head held high, the Fjeld horse pulled the McCormick down the outside edge of the field. A six foot swath followed and the heavy headed bundles came off, tumbling down the elevated structure ready to be stacked in shocks. The noise from the small crowd gathered rose in admiration and appreciation for machine, horse and Nels.

"Put me on your calendar, a week from today. That ought to give those heads time to ripen just enough. I'll come to the shop and we'll talk cost," shouted Harmen, louder than necessary. "Won't have to hire that part done. Less worry from weather, too, I'd guess."

Harmen's field was the first of ten on Nels' schedule. "You be able to finish all your bookings? How do you know how long each field will take?" questioned Alex when Nels brought the horse and binder back to the stable where Alex was cutting a maple log.

"Land is flat here. The McCormick is new and shouldn't need repairs. Eric has a new sickle blade to replace the one in the machine when I need a sharper one. The only thing I worry about is "winter potatoes" in the fields. Can't see them too well with the grain as tall as it is."

"Winter potatoes? Never heard of those kind before. Good to eat?"

"Alex, that's why I enjoy you around," chuckled Nels. "Winter potatoes are what some farmers call large rocks. Don't think you'd even care to cook them, unless you need one as a griddle to fry your corn bread. Some of the local farmers pick rocks. Others think since the rocks come up on their own from the frost and freezing of the ground, they will somehow disappear. You've noticed I've been conveniently busy when one or two of the menfolk have come by to ask if I'd harvest for them. When I know they don't pick rocks, I'm not willing to harvest their field. Too much can happen to the McCormick. It's not worth the chance of damage to the machine." Taking his mug down from its peg where it hung on the wall, Nels filled his cup from the coffee pot he always had brewing sitting on the back of the stove. Even in the late summer heat, Nels made a small fire just for that purpose. He was sure no good Norskie could live without an ample supply of coffee available. "That the last spoon, Alex?"

"Sure is. The wild rose carving on the handles of the wood mixing spoons are so much easier to do than those vines Mrs. Primrose wanted."

"She been here again, Alex?"

"Just this morning. She must watch out her kitchen window so she's aware of your coming and going. Her new house is next to yours, right?"

"I built Sophie's house about five years ago, long before she even thought of coming west. Had I known Primrose'd stay and build next door, I would have bought that little piece of land too."

"You could always put up a wood fence," offered Alex.

"It would take too much lumber to make it high enough so her nose wouldn't see and . . ." Interrupted by the loud unexpected ringing of the church bell, both men rushed out into the street. Billowing clouds of smoke came from the area west, beyond the railroad tracks.

"Fire! Fire! Need help!"

Men scrambled to grab their shovels, rakes and gunny sacks. Nels ran to the stable and hitched Stout to his cart. He drove west down the street slow enough so that those armed could jump aboard. "How bad?" he asked anyone in particular.

"Not good. Lars had his grain down but not in bundles. Train came through. Cinders from the boiler must have spewed out through the smokestack and started the fire."

Stopping long enough to let the men off, he stated, "I'll be back. I'll see if I can give others a ride out." Stout wheeled and galloped with the cart behind as best he could back to the stable. Nels didn't stop there but went to the east end of town where he saw others running, rakes and shovels in hand. Wheeling again, he slowed Stout enough so that those wanting to hop on the cart could. Same question was asked, "How bad is it, Nels? Can it be stopped?"

"Seen this before. Only way to stop a range fire is to backfire it. I'm going to skirt the outside of the cut field and go a safe distance so that you can spread out. Jacob, take charge. You've done this before."

"Stop here," ordered Jacob. Stout felt the slight backward pull on the reins and did just that. As the men and young boys dismounted, they heard Jacob say, "If we work fast, we can save half of Lars' downed crop. Those of you who can move the fastest, go as far down to the west as his crop lies down. I think there's a water gully somewhere not far down there. Dig a trench. Start the fire and let it spread towards what is already burning. When you have it started, kill the initial burning closest to you. Be careful. Flames will be hot. This wheat is dry from lying. It will ignite easily. Likes pants legs!"

Those with shovels dug a trench. Others lit the backfire and made sure that what was burning did not jump the trench. Quick hands saw results. Clouds of smoke became smoldering embers across a blackened land. Returning with women this time, Nels stopped by the small groups now leaning on their handles. The women offered grateful drinks of water to the overheated firefighters from the dippers in the large crocks. With thirsts sated and the fire squelched, Nels reloaded the ladies, and Norris whose pant leg had caught fire. "Come with us, Norris. Doc's waiting in case he's needed. The sooner you get his burn ointment on that, the better it will feel." I'll be back for the rest of you men.

21 Help

Footsteps heard on the stairs alerted Sara that she would soon have a visitor. Setting aside her embroidery on the baptismal gown ordered, she waited to see who would come in her door. "Mrs. Larson. Is the rent due? I'm so busy I tend to lose track of the days."

"No Sara. I'm not here collecting. We are sending in an order for dry goods on tomorrow's train east. Wondered if you would help me choose some velvets and wools suitable for more dressy clothing. We're getting ready for the winter season and need to buy ahead so we are sure that the order will arrive on time."

"I'd be glad to help, Mrs. Larson. Let me finish tying off this embroidery thread and I'll be down. I haven't put the 'Will Be Back Soon' sign on my door in a long time. It's good to have an excuse to do so."

"Come to the back room of the store. I have all the samples there. Also have a fresh berry pie. We'll have coffee first and then see what you think we should order." All business, she left as quickly as she came.

"Ouch!" Sara stuck her left pointer finger in her mouth to stave the flow of blood, if any. Always when she needed to hurry, caution seemed to leave her. Blood stains, anywhere on a garment were difficult to remove. Lowering her finger and wiping it on a rag she kept for just that purpose, Sara gently pressed on the area. No blood came. Quickly, she finished her task, checked her hair in the mirror, found it serviceable, and hastened down the stairs with her sign in hand. Placing the sign on its peg, she shut the door and found her way to the back room of the Dry Goods Store. Her mouth watered as she entered. A sweet smell of fresh baked cherry pie greeted her.

"Sit here, "Mrs. Larson gestured. "Please call me Clara. I'm not used to the being called Mrs. by my friends and I consider you a special one. Sophie and I were very close, having come here about the same time. I miss her."

"Uncle Nels and I miss her too."

"Thought about getting some help, Sara. You are spending too many late nights for a young person like you finishing those orders."

"I have. I am not sure how to go about hiring someone."

"Some 'motherly' advice. Think about telling Pastor Deacon that you are interested in hiring someone. You'll need to be specific, what kind of help you need."

"When I first came, Clara, Aunt Sophie was to sew the simpler items people ordered. I was to design and make the patterns for the more intricate stitching."

"Sara, finding that sort of person shouldn't be

that difficult. Most women out here grow up learning to sew at a very young age."

"Learning to sew and running a sewing machine like I have two of isn't that simple. Most don't even own a machine. Harder than that is to find someone to do the fine stitching needed which the machine can't do. Fine sewing takes practice and some skill."

"Why not ask Pastor to collect samples of sewing from the ladies who might be interested. I think he'd do that for you, Sara. That way you can see for yourself which one would best suit your need."

"Once we make some choices of fabric to order, I'll go over and talk to him if he is in. If I don't take action when the idea is fresh, I set it aside and don't get at it. It's a flaw in my character that I've had to deal with all of my life."

Pie enjoyed and selections made, Sara found her way to the parsonage. When she knocked on the door, little Amy opened it, turned back towards the kitchen and yelled, "Ma, Sara's here. Did you order a new dress for me?"

"Tell her to come in. I'll be there in a minute."

"Amy, looks like you finally lost that front tooth that's been slow to pop out."

"I did, Sara. Mom fixed corn on the cob last night. First bite and it was out."

"Good. That means you won't have to see Doctor Spillum and have him get it out for you." Aware of Mrs. Deacon's entry into the room, Sara stood, and held out her hand. "Mrs. Deacon. Does your husband happen to be here? I have a favor to ask of him, but maybe you could help me as well."

"I'd be glad to help, Sara, if it doesn't entail sewing. I am the world's worst."

"Well it does, in a way. I am in need of hiring someone to help me at the shop. I know so few people and most of those are the ones that I have sewn for. I seem so busy that I am unable to gather when the women meet for Bible studies or women's work for the church. Mrs. Larson suggested I come to pastor and see if he could help. She thought that in his and your conversations with the locals and your parishioners, you or he might discover someone who was looking for extra work and could sew a good seam."

"That is very possible, especially when we have the quilters meet. Do you want me to announce at the next meeting on Monday that you are looking for someone?"

"No. We, Clara and I, thought it might be better if anyone interested would supply a sample, and leave it in my mailbox at the Dry Goods Shop. That way I could look at the work, see its quality and decide if the person would be a good employee."

"I'm not sure what kind of response that will bring from our parishioners here but we'll try it that way. If no one responds, we may have to put the word out at Pastor's other parish that he serves. Off hand, I can think of two younger girls who may be interested. Both are sixteen, I think, and are the oldest in large families. In both cases, there is another baby on the way and little room in those small cabins for more children. Parents of either girls may be very glad to have their daughter come and work for a good Christian like you. I'll see what I can find out about each of them."

"Thank you for your help. I must be going. I have 'Back Soon' sign on my door to the shop so I can't be gone long." Sara watched as Amy whispered in her mother's ear.

"No, Amy. I'm sorry. We haven't the money for a new dress just yet. You will have to wait a while," came from a mother, a little embarrassed and finding it hard to deny her only child a wish.

Sensing the pain in the mother's words, Sara spoke again. "Mrs. Deacon. Next time you are by my shop, please bring Amy up. I have some yardage left over from another project that I did. I'd love to make it into a Christmas dress for her."

"Oh, dear. We would be so grateful. She is growing so fast as you can see. Most of her dresses are too small. People are good to give us food but few think about clothing. Pastor and I will help you make a choice in who to hire if you will let us."

"Any help I can get will be most appreciated. And, when I make that dress, I will be sure to allow for growth," offered Sara as she let herself out of the door and headed back to her shop.

22 Free Time

Uncle Nels brought home a large basket one day that he'd somehow either found or bought at the mercantile, Sara never did find out which. He insisted that she participate in the church basket social.

"When do I have time to fry chicken, make any cookies and bake bread? You know that we eat soup most of the time."

"Sara, there's more to life than sewing. This is a chance to have some good fun. Want to come riding with me? My roan needs exercise and so does Stout. When is your new helper coming? It can't be soon enough, girl."

"Riding? Uncle Nels, are you trying to tell me something? Sick of me living here? If so, I'll get a room at the Marta's house or rent the back part of my sewing shop and convert it to living quarters. It is storage for the dry goods store now but could be adapted to my needs, I'd think."

"My dear, I'm not wanting you to move. Certainly not to that drafty room at back of the shop. Sophie complained about the cold coming from that back part when she was alive."

"Sorry, I am tired. Orders keep coming in and I can't seem to turn people down, not even the prissy Mrs. Primrose who now orders dresses and suits to match the hats she makes," shared Sara, turning and hugging her uncle. "Emma, the girl I've hired, needs to wait to come here until her mother has the new baby. She is the oldest and feels responsible. She'll come to work for me when her mother is strong enough to care for everyone. Emma's five siblings are all much younger than she."

"The basket?"

Walking to the stairway that led to her bedroom, she stopped just before climbing. "Put it on the counter there. I'll put something in it, not sure what," decided Sara. "Don't tell Alex. He's already been asking."

Alex had asked if she was bringing a basket when she met him in front of the Dry Goods Store just yesterday morning. Sara had evaded his questioning, not sure of how she felt about him and not having a basket to spare. Though the church was fairly newly built, Alex told her that the roof leaked around the piping for the pot belly stove and needed fixing. Not having been a part of a basket social, Sara had asked, "What happens at one of these socials, Alex?"

"Sara, you've seen the signs up in many of the shops, I'm sure, instructing the women, married or not, to decorate a picnic box or basket. I'm told that Lucas will auction off the boxes and baskets. The highest bidder on each box will have the privilege of sharing the noon meal with the owner of the basket."

"Do they make much money doing this?"

"Hope is that a certain box or two would interest bidders enough so that the price to see whose box it is and what is in it would bring more money for that one than most."

"So that's why you want to know. Afraid you'll have to eat with someone who can't cook, Alex?"

"I've not been to such a social either, Sara. If I'm going to spend my hard earned money, I'd like to be sure it's worth every penny."

"First I need a basket. Then, I'll see what I can find to put in it" and she hurried on up to her shop.

Sara never thought that Uncle Nels would be the person to make a basket so available. Now she had little choice.

"She making a picnic basket for the raffle, Nels?" Rufus asked when Nels came to take his roan out for a run.

"I've told her about the raffle and supplied a basket. It's something she's never done. She's lived a pretty sheltered life. She's worried about who she'd have to share her meal with."

"We can fix that. Tell Henry or Alex what her basket looks like and they'll bid for it, I'm sure."

"Think I'll let the good Lord take care of this problem. He'll make a better decision than I ever could. I'm riding west to exercise this roan. He becomes pretty skittish if I don't ride him regularly. Should be back around noon if anyone asks for me, Rufus." Nels headed the roan down the old oxcart trail by the river, curious to see if the trail was still used. The overhang of branches where there were trees gave welcoming shade from the hot sun that beat down. Hearing rustling in front of him, he slowed the horse and cautiously moved forward. A small herd of eight deer stood in the clearing just to his left. Being downwind from the herd, the sentinel of the herd had not sensed the horse with its rider. Drawing his rifle from its place by the saddle horn, Nels took aim and killed a young doe. The noise of the rifle startled the herd and they scattered immediately in all directions. Alighting, Nels took the reins and tied his roan to a nearby tree and walked cautiously to his kill. Dead it was from a shot through the neck. "Glad this is no more than a two year old. Any heavier and I'd have trouble getting it up in front of me so I can get it back home," voiced Nels, knowing no one heard him. Untying the reins from the tree and wrapping them around the pommel, he stepped to the side of the horse and grabbed the pommel once again. In one smooth motion, Nels mounted into the saddle, and moved the roan closer to the doe. Once there, he stepped down and attached the rope to the front quarters. Mounting the roan again, he carefully hoisted his kill up and settled the deer comfortably in front of him for the short trip back home. Rufus saw him coming and stopped his never ending task of filling the water troughs.

"What do you have, Nels?"

"Nice young doe from a herd of eight just north of here on the old trail by the river. I need to let it hang somewhere before I cut it up. You willing to let it hang in the stable once we take care of the innards? Don't think the ladies coming to buy furniture would be too happy to see it hanging in my shop."

"Take it to the back to that enclosed area. Should be fine there. I'll be in to help you soon as I finish filling the tanks for the next train due soon. Use those sawhorses standing in the corner."

"I'll take some of the rough cut lumber that I haven't been able to use and make a table."

"I'll come and help you, Nels, after the Limited comes and goes. I hear it so it shouldn't be too long before I'm there."

Nels moved his roan into the stable and back to the area Rufus indicated and eased the doe to the stall floor. Taking the roan back to its stall, he hung a feed bag filled with a good portion of oats over the ears of the horse and walked back to the empty stall. The sawhorses were easy to spot up against the wall. He dragged them out into the lighted area of the stall and positioned them to support the boards he knew were stacked in his area. Selecting four of the roughest cut, he carried them two at a time and placed them on the sawhorses. Once the table was ready, he half dragged and half carried the awkward critter over to the table and hoisted it up. Returning to the horse, he removed the feed bag and took him to the watering trough, let him drink his fill and put him back in his stall. Removing the bridle and saddle, he grabbed the brush and curried the places where both had been. Just as he finished with the roan, the train whistle blew and Nels knew it was leaving.

"Brought these, Nels. Thought we might need them."

"Good, Rufus, just got done stabling the roan. Hadn't got that far ahead to think about where we were going to put any of the innards we'll save. The two small pans will do for the heart and liver. The larger one will hold the intestines we'll clean and save so they can be used for sausage casings." The two worked side by side slitting the belly open and removing the parts wanted and tossing the rest. Once the inside was gutted, Rufus tied a rope around the hind legs and threw the other end over a beam overhead. The two struggled to hoist the doe in the air enough so the head cleared the dirt floor. Satisfied that the doe was secure, the two worked on cleaning the intestines, making sure they were well rinsed.

"About done, I think," offered Rufus.

"Think so. Here, you take the heart and the liver. Never did like either one. I'm sure Sara doesn't either. Need any of the casings?"

"No, but I bet Jon wouldn't mind having them. It's hunting season and he'll make lots of sausage."

"Good idea. I'm past the sausage making stage of my life. Too much work. Rather buy a piece or two from Jon. I'll see he gets them."

Looking at his time piece in his vest pocket, Rufus said, "Time to get cleaned up for the basket social. Hope I get a good basket. Don't care really who the woman is. I'm more interested in the food than tangling with a woman."

23 Basket

    The picnic box decorated with a brightly striped ribbon was packed with fried chicken, a loaf of whole wheat bread, sweet creamed butter and a dozen spritz cookies – food enough for two.
    The grey suit that she'd traveled here in on the train when she first left the Nordic mountains had long since lost its stiffness and fashion. If she were to be respected as a seamstress, she knew she had to display her skills. Making this new, skirted dress was one way to demonstrate the eastern magazine styles. Besides, she was tired of wearing all that fluff underneath her skirts to make them billow at the hemline. Her very thin waist didn't need the laced undergarment either. She'd even asked Mrs. Primrose to make a hat to complete the outfit. Sara wondered when she first saw the hat whether it was a way of making her the laughing stock of the little berg when

she mingled with the people.

Then, she saw other orders of hats waiting to be retrieved. Similar styled hats were lying on the work table, all obviously ordered by women for this same

occasion, and made much like hers. Sara noticed that Priscilla had used some remnants of fabric from the dresses Sara had sewn for her customers to make matching hats for them. Feeling like she had wings on the top of her head, Sara carefully used a hatpin and pinned the hat to her hair. She slid the thin bit of elastic attached to the hat under her bun, perching the hat just above the bun of softly braided blond hair and went down to wait for Nels and the cart. Boarding the cart that Nels had ready for her, Sara stepped up and carefully seated herself so the dress she'd purposely made for this occasion didn't wrinkle. She waited as Nels climbed in beside her. Feeling the cart settle with his cargo, Stout moved forward without Nels' direction.

Reaching church, the horse stopped in front of the walkway that lead to the church steps. Nels told Sara purposely to go ahead to where the ladies were gathering, hoping that those anxious to speak with her would ignore him and the basket they'd tucked under the seat out of view. He hurried Stout and the cart out of the way of others wanting to unload their families. Nels stepped down and staked Stout and the small two seated cart in a grassy area at the side of the church. Tucking the small basket under his arm so that the ribbon was not visible, Nels moved towards the end of a table, set the basket down on the its end and moved on to where Harmen and others were standing deep in conversation.

Lars stepped out of the group, extended his hand and put his other hand on Nels shoulder as he spoke. "Never did get a chance to thank you for saving the rest of the crop the day of the fire. Bringing the men and positioning them so they could backfire meant I lost some of the downed wheat, sure. I'd have lost it all without the backfiring," came in a voice unsteady with emotion. "Had I lost it all, I'd have lost the farm."

"Sara said you'd come by when I was out with the McCormick west of here," said Nels as he took the hand offered, feeling the firmness in the gratitude not only from the voice but from the strength of the fingers as they grasped his hand. " We are so lucky."

"Machine makes a difference," Harmen added.

"Winds in the last years have picked up the dried grain spears and scattered them so that shocking what is redistributed by those winds is not easy. The heavy ripened grain heads come off so easily when they are jostled by wind and the yield is less. I want you to sign me up for next year. Unless the hoppers come, I'll not risk another train disaster like this one could have been. Ever think about running another rig? Seems like you were pretty busy this year. I know some did not have a chance to hire you."

"Eric and I have talked about it, for sure. Rocks are always such a problem for the McCormick. Unless all the farmers are willing to pick, we're not going to be too willing to come and harvest. Too much time gets wasted in repairing the machine." Not wanting to commit ahead of time, Nels changed the subject. "Heard from my son. I understand he may come here. Not sure how that will go."

"Why's that Nels? He hard to get along with?"

"No, when I left, he took over my furniture business. With large companies manufacturing furniture now, there isn't so much sale for individual pieces. But Nelson has always had other interests. He has a herd of Reds he's bringing with him. One of my uncles owns a large herd and Nelson has worked for him when he's not been busy making furniture. He's going to put the Reds on the train like we did Stout."

"Reds? Reds what? Hope it's not sheep," declared Lars.

"Sheep? Did I hear sheep? Hope no one brings any of those critters out this way. They'll destroy our good grazing land here. We don't have that much to spare," announced Andrew, a cheese maker who had his own herd of cattle on a small farm near Goose.

"No, Andy, sounds like you've got competition coming?"

"What's this? Competition? Another cheese maker?"

"No, not a cheese maker. Nelson never learned that trade. The women back home always made the cheese. My son's bringing a herd of the Norwegian Red cattle our family has always raised since we move out of Bergen and into the mountains above." "He have land here around Goose?" questioned Andy, still concerned about the pressure another herd might have on his sales of milk, cream, cheese and butter.

"No, our family has had a homestead north and west of here around Georgetown. Our great uncle, Bjorn, was one of the first to settle in that area."

"No one on it?"

"Oh, yes. It's been share cropped since his death but the family that has always been there found a homestead that they are buying. Nelson has thoughts that this is the 'Land of Milk and Honey' like so much of the advertisements say and wants to come."

"He's going to take the herd there?" uttered Andy, with a hopeful sigh in his voice.

"Ja. I'm anxious too. Haven't seen him since I left – let's see – twelve or so years ago, I guess. Neither of us is good to write either," chuckled Nels. "Letters come and go once or twice a year."

"Hard to have cattle shipped over. How many is he . . ." Andy's attempt to learn more about the Reds came to a halt with the church bell ringing loudly.

Pastor Deacon stepped to the front of the group that was seated at tables in an open gathering area opposite where the horses were tied to the rails. "Time to auction off the lovely baskets, gentlemen. Be generous with your bidding. The roof hole around the smoke stack isn't getting any better. Don't need more damage from water. Lucas, come and get the bidding started." Taking one of the bigger baskets from the center of the table, Lucas started the auction. "Picked this bigger one, men. Some of you have large appetites. This looks like it holds a whole chicken. Smells like it too. Heavy enough to be packing two chickens. What do I hear offered for this basket?" Men gathered close and competitive bidding started. It didn't seem like the look of the basket made any difference. Who was bidding against another caused the competitiveness.

Sara stood in back and waited anxiously for her basket to be auctioned, worrying all the while who she would have to share her noon meal with. Looking around, she spotted some of the locals who continuously visited the saloon. Her box was on the end of a table. Lucas seemed to be working his way from the middle of the table to the outer edges. For this, Sara was grateful. "The saloon men must be hungry," she whispered to Marta standing next to her.

"Be glad of that, Sara. Means you won't have to eat with one of them. You brought a basket I hope?"

"I did. Uncle Nels set it on the edge of the table."

"He did you a favor. He's been to one of these auctions before, never seems to be too anxious to bid but is always anxious to eat," giggled Marta.

"I know why," Sara offered. "I can cook. Problem is I have little time to make a good meal as busy as I am at the shop."

"You've a young girl coming to help, I hear. Ingrid will miss Emma. Needs to stop having all those young ones! Suppose it doesn't do any good to tell her that." "Pastor and Mrs. Deacon were so good to help me. I knew I needed to hire someone but had no idea how to decide who it might be. Oh, look, that's my basket," came from Sara. This was the first that she'd spotted Alex. He had worked his way closer to Lucas, filling in a spot here and there when the high bidder retrieved the basket he'd bought. She watched Alex move from the center and walk to the outside edge where he now stood waiting for the rest of the boxes to sell.

Bidding on the box Alex decided to buy started slowly until Henry and another person he had not seen before realized that Alex was bidding seriously on the basket Lucas had in hand.

"Does Alex know it's yours?" whispered Marta.

"Not that I know of."

"Wouldn't be a bad match for you, Sara. He seems so aware of other's needs. He's been raised well."

Sara heard none of this motherly advice as she focused on the bidding and the bidders. Who was that roughly dressed, long straggly haired person so intent on having her box? And Henry, now also determined that this box be his lunch!

"Looks like we have some real competition for this box," interjected Lucas as he accepted the bids from the three. In the end, Alex had the last say and the prized basket was handed to him. "Does this mean that you're interested in the cook too, Alex?" questioned Lucas. Alex blushed, something unusual for him and the crowd roared in laughter. Sara was glad she had stood at the back of the crowd and that they were unaware of her red face.

"Not sure whose it is but I do smell that chicken," and he stepped back to the side and waited while the few remaining baskets sold.

"Here's the last one."

"Glad mine's not the last one sold," declared Mrs. Primrose in a loud enough voice so many around heard the derogatory tone she used. Having to deal with people placed in embarrassing financial situations, Lucas was quick to react. "Sorry to disappoint the rest of you men. I am offering twenty-five dollars for this one. I'm hungry. Anyone want to up the offer? Harmen, how about you?"

"Already have one, remember."

"Anyone else willing to up the ante?" Peeking inside, he continued. "Last, Mrs. Primrose does not necessarily mean worst!" Waiting as the giggles quieted, he continued, "You're missing out on a good meal, men. Willing to bid against me? Hearing none, the auction is closed. Give Parson Deacon your money before you eat. That way what you get in the box to eat or the person with whom you share your meal with won't affect your willingness to pay. Remember, Deacon will be eating his box up here at this table, so when you're done eating, he'll accept any tips for the good food."

Men waited as women approached them, claiming each basket bought. Alex stood waiting patiently for his "cook" to come forward, wondering too what he'd gotten himself in for. Whoever it was seemed reluctant to come and retrieve her basket. Was it possible the person would refuse to claim the basket?

He stood to the side of the auction table with others – holding one of the six baskets that had not been "claimed." Then he spotted Sara moving toward the group. Could he have been that lucky? Was it her basket? He looked at the remaining men. Three had walked away with their partners. The rest stood with him and waited. He saw Nels out of the corner of his eye, as concerned as Alex was that the one remaining saloon man was not to be Sara's meal mate. The other was an elderly man who had just come off the west bound train this morning. "I should be like Mrs. Primrose. By now I'd know the old guy's family history! Hope it's Miss Prissy's basket he gets," thought Alex with a smirk on his face. So absorbed was he in his thoughts about the new visitor that he did not realize his basket in hand was the last to be claimed. Sara was heading towards him with concern on her face.

Though she had little time to cook, when she had, and Alex had been invited to share a meal, he praised her cooking skills and told her that whatever she'd made was very good. Usually that day of invitation had been through Nels on Sunday after church. The dress shop was closed on Sunday as all shops were Sundays except for the hotel. Marta didn't cook noon or evening meals for her boarders on Sunday. Those staying at her house had no choice if they wanted to eat except to go to the hotel's dining room for any meals. Even the Saloon's doors were closed, unusual for most western towns where trains stopped.

Wringing her hands, Sara looked up at his grinning face and asked, "How did you know?"

"Didn't Sara, I swear. Must have had an angel guiding me." Taking her arm at the elbow, he offered, "Let's find a place to sit away from the rest." Carrying the basket gingerly in his other hand, he continued, "Wait here, please, while I go pay Deacon for my prize." Alex wondered why the elderly gentleman kept following him but decided not to waste his time away from Sara. "He's a fine young man, Sara," offered Marta as she came by on the way to her lunch partner.

She'd waited to join her partner and stood, watching the two. "Nels is paying for mine." She walked away with firmness in her step and a smile on her face, thinking she too was lucky. In Marta's mind, Nels was a special man and needed a woman's companionship besides his niece Sara. "I need to set aside more time for him," she thought as she moved in his direction.

Alex returned just as the lady with the stranger came towards them. Unwilling to share his time with Sara, Alex stepped in front of them and shielded Sara from any contact. He took her elbow again and turned her towards the river bank, a ways away from the church but still visible to anyone curious. Finding a level place on the river bank to sit down away from the crowd, Alex watched as Sara carefully adjusted the skirt of her dress beneath her so it would not wrinkle or get too grass stained. Silence surrounded them. A single chirp or two came from a bird or a squirrel. Too far away from any of the crowd now to hear any conversations, Sara saw that the gathered people either shared their box lunches or found satisfaction in the pea soup the church women had cooked earlier in the morning and was now available.

Sara opened her basket, took out the cloth she'd brought and spread it on the tufted grass between them. Next came the carefully wrapped chicken pieces. Behind it came the wheat bread she'd remembered to slice into thick slabs and the creamed butter. "Sorry, Alex. Didn't bring plates either. I've never sold a lunch basket before. Never even knew of this tradition for raising funds. Probably wouldn't have filled one today either except Uncle Nels insisted I have some fun. I wasn't sure it would be fun. Knew it would take time away from my sewing. Made him promise to stay close if some saloon guy bought my basket. Good thing I did. I was worried about that stranger with a hat. Did you see him? And those other two ruffians you stood with at the end. I didn't know whether I should run or trust Uncle Nels to stay close." Alex let her rattle on, sensing her nervousness. "The small chokecherry jelly jar stands on the counter by the sink. Never found its way into the basket. I know you like sweets."

"To share this basket with you is sweet," spoke Alex in a soft, heartfelt voice as he carefully placed his hand on her wrist.

As though in her own world and not hearing him, she continued, "I did pack extra napkins. Here's one." Reaching into the basket, she carefully brought it out and handed it to him. Opening the cloth with the wrapped chicken, she offered Alex his choice of pieces.

"Mmmm. Every time you fix chicken at your cabin, how is it that your chicken is always crisp on the outside and moist on the inside? What Marta cooks at the boarding house is dry and tough to chew."

"Probably because she has to make so much of it at one time. The only way she can keep the quantity she needs to fix to satisfy all of you warm is to put it in the oven. That's why it dries out and gets tough."

"Smells good," offered Alex.

Reaching in again and this time leaving the chicken on the cloth between them she said, "Here's more. Eat your fill. What isn't eaten I'll send back to Marta's with you for a late night snack. I know she doesn't cook for you on Sundays so you need to go to the hotel to eat if you are hungry. You can always return the basket."

"Sara, relax. You've hardly eaten anything. I know this is a new experience. It is for me too. I've never even bid on a lunch basket, let along bought one. I promise not to be any different today than I have been to you any other time that we've been together."

"I'm so sorry, Alex. I am acting like a youngster, I know. I haven't spent much time alone with men, especially anyone as kind hearted as you have been, helping me whenever you could with all the heavy boxes that come in shipped on the train. I was so uneasy about who I'd have to eat with, especially when I saw that strange man standing on the side. I was so worried until you started biding. You spent a lot of your cash.

"I did. Had a good reason too. I didn't come here thinking I'd buy a basket. My thought in doing so as I stood there watching the auction was that I haven't been a good church person, not giving much to God. The church roof is a sorry mess and does need work. Nels and I intend to see what we can do about it tomorrow. Now that his harvesting is over, he has time on his hands again. No sense in making more furniture until we sell what we have or get orders. We decided to wait until after today and the auction so that everyone felt the need to spend the money to see it fixed before we started fixing it. Thought the auction would raise more money that way. Now I'm rambling. Can't let this chicken go to waste," and he reached for the last leg on the cloth.

Sara looked out, wondering if Uncle Nels had stayed close and was watching them. Spotting him down on the bank of the river to the left of them, she exclaimed with joy, "Look, Alex. Uncle Nels bought Marta's basket."

"Doesn't surprise me."

"Why do you say that? You must know more than I do about those two."

"Only what I've heard Marta say now and again. Sometimes when you are busy, Nels comes over at noon to have lunch with those of us who are boarders and come back to claim our noon meal. She sets us at the large table in her dining room. The side board is laden with whatever she had fixed and we are free to eat as much as we want. Nels always comes just a little late. When he comes, she hands him a plate. The two of them fill their plates and take them back to the kitchen. Haven't thought about their actions too much until I saw the bidding today and watched Nels. He had no interest in any basket but one. The basket Marta brought was sitting on the side board yesterday."

"Aren't there other singles staying at the house? Couldn't they have seen the basket? Certainly you could have."

"Other singles stay there but most are older women. I was watching you to see if I could tell if you had brought a basket. When yours came up, I saw Marta and you whispering. Your actions gave me hope that this basket was yours." Wiping his face and hands with his napkin and folding it, Alex leaned back on an elbow. "Are you ready for all the activity that will come on the train?"

"What activity is that, Alex? You do know something about that man that bought a basket, don't you?"

"No, he's a mystery to me though I'll see what I can find out. He's dressed well. That should mean he has a purpose for being here if he stays beyond today."

"The only activity I'm aware of is that Nelson is bringing a herd of cows and taking them up to the land Uncle Nels inherited up near Georgetown east and north of here on the Red River. His great uncle, Bjorn, left him a sizable homestead in a will. Nelson should be here any day now unless he had trouble with the Reds. Shouldn't have. Most Reds are even tempered. Don't know why his wouldn't be," revealed Sara still gnawing on a chicken wing in between sentences and gently wiping her mouth and fingers now and then.

"A passenger left a New York paper on the train that came through this morning and the conductor gave it to me. Front page story is about Teddy Roosevelt trying to save the Badlands. He sure is stirring up interest in those hills. The Easterners who are curious will come on the train out west for their vacations to stay near his ranch and see those beautiful hills and buttes out in the Dakotas."

"You ever seen the Badlands, Alex?"

"A part of them on the east end. Never been as far as what some call the Wild West. Rugged country. Strange small mountains called buttes, high hills really, that have flat tops and were formed from water rushing around them sometime eons ago when this area was flooded. I remember you said you miss mountains. I haven't seen what I'd call mountains, having lived around here all my life. Maybe the two of us could ride the train way out west one day. The Limited is supposed to go through some of that rugged country when it gets out of this flat land on its way to the west coast.

Sara didn't know what he meant about riding the train with him. Certainly she'd have to have a chaperone. It wouldn't be proper otherwise so she changed the subject as her mother had taught her to do when she wanted to not answer a pointed or difficult question. "Want more bread, Alex?"

"Think I'm full. Thanks for taking the time to fix the basket," he said as he sat up thinking she was anxious to go back.

Sara started to gather wrappings and realized the basket had another covered package. "We're not done. I have spritz cookies. I almost forgot."

Grateful for the cookies to sate his sweet tooth but more grateful for the extended time it would take to eat them, Alex leaned back on his elbow once again.

Two questions came from Sara between cookie nibbles. "What do you know about this Roosevelt person? Think he's an honest man?"

"Have to wait and see. Hope more of the papers come this way on the train and someone leaves them so I get a chance to read them. I've asked the conductor to save any papers he sees."

"Wish I could vote when the time comes. Even if women could vote, I've a long ways to go before I could have that privilege. I don't even have my citizenship papers. You have yours, I suppose." Sara sat quietly and waited for Alex to answer.

"I was born here. My mother and my grandparents on her side of the family live in St. Paul. Haven't seen either of them since last summer this time. Years before, I've gotten on one of the boats headed down the Goose to where it meets the Mississippi and on down to St. Paul to spend a week or two with them. Now I could ride the train. Nels has kept me so busy that

I haven't thought about making that trip this year. 'Sides, since I'm not going to cut wood this winter, it hasn't crossed my mind that I should make the trip."

"And your father?"

"He died in one of the battles in the Spanish American War. His folks, my other set of grandparents on my father's side are still in Sweden, very aged but still living."

"Sweden? You're Swedish? Oh, my. Can't wait until I tell Uncle Nels." Sara giggled and went on, "To think that he hired a Swede! His family will never give him peace if they find out!" Gathering her skirt in her left hand, she extended the other to Alex. "Help me up, please. I see Uncle Nels has unhitched Stout from his post. Looks like he is returning to the livery. My new shoes are tight. I don't want to have to walk back." Standing and straightening her skirt, Sara took the basket in hand, smiled at Alex and thanked him for spending his money on her lunch. As the two reached the cart, Alex saw to her stepping up and being seated by Nels.

"Hope you had as good a noon meal as I did, Nels. Enjoyed my company immensely. Let me know if Nelson comes and he needs help with the herd. Train's about due from the east. I'm going to see if I can help Deacon carry tables back in church. I'll stop by the livery before I go back to Marta's."

The train whistle blew announcing its arrival. "Hop on the back Alex. Think I hear cattle bawling. Might be Nelson and the Reds." Alex did as he was told and Stout trotted out at a good pace, anxious to be back at the stable and the oats he knew he'd get once back in his stall.

24 Family

The group of Reds Nelson called a herd was small by many standards here in the west. Twenty cattle stirred uneasily in a make-shift corral next to the water tower and wood pile. With cattle bawling, reacting to the new surroundings and wanting to be fed, Nelson did not hear the horse and cart come. Sara was the first off the cart and raced towards him.

"Nelson, you've grown," came from the startled Sara who reached to hug him.

"Sara, that you?" Sara had no time to answer. The train blew its whistle as a signal it was leaving and the agitated cattle broke loose from their rope holdings and began to scatter through the streets. Taking Stout's reins freed from the harness of the cart, Alex bounded on the horse, riding bareback style.

"Watch, Nelson," Sara proudly announced. "He and Stout will get them back."

Impatiently waiting and putting trust in this new friend of Sara's, Nelson stood by her and watched. "I forgot you took Stout with you. I wasn't happy when I heard that. I'd used him so much in driving the cattle up and down the mountain to new feeding grounds. He's good."

Good he was. In no time the cattle were back but this time Alex guided them to the livery stable where he knew there were extra stalls. Nels was waiting.

"Who's he, Sara? Good cattleman, I think," came from Nelson, quick to judge people by action and reaction.

"Far as I know, he's a woodcutter. Has been carving for Uncle Nels when someone orders furniture that they want fancied."

"Been around long?"

"Since the spring thaw and didn't go back this fall when his crew stopped, heading north to the timberland to cut logs and lumber."

"Probably see you tonight," Nelson said, turning towards the stable. "I better go see what Pa intends, herding the cattle into the livery. Better see if he's got room enough to keep them for a day or two. I'd like to let them settle down before I try to drive them to Georgetown, wherever that is from here."

Left to her own, Sara headed back to her shop, intent on finishing a shirt she was making for Alex. Marta told her that his birthday was this coming Wednesday and she was making a cake to celebrate. Sara promised she'd make a special effort to have noon meal with the boarding house crew that day. Lifting her skirts to insure she wouldn't trip on the hem, she gingerly stepped up each of the steps on the stairs, glad when the top one was reached. New shoes were not fun to wear, even the soft leather ones she'd sent for from the catalogue Clara lent her, a catalogue that the dry goods store ordered from all the time.

Taking the shirt from her stack of sewing on a small table next to her machine by the window, Sara wished she were at Uncle Nels and her bedroom there so she could change from the dress she wore. Instead, she sat and unlaced her shoes, glad that she always kept an extra pair here at the shop in case of rain. Rain and the mud from the street had ruined one pair of new shoes and she was determined not to let that happen again. "Wish it would rain. I'd be glad to take these new shoes out and let the rain gently fall on them. Might stretch the leather a little bit and make them more comfortable." The noise from the sack race in the street below distracted her. Pastor Deacon had quickly organized a race as one of the activities to keep the younger ones busy while the parents shared their lunchboxes. As she watched, six pairs of varying aged young people readied at the starting line. A small hand gun was fired and the pairs hopped, fell, got back in position in the sacks and hopped some more. Prize was a silver dollar, worth a few bruises and bloodshed Two small but sturdy girls won. "Must have practiced," mumbled Sara proudly and she turned her attention to the detailing around the shirt pocket.

Dusk settled on Goose and Sara set the completed shirt aside, leaving it handy so she'd remember to press it in the morning. Finding her shoe bag in the bottom of the only closet in the shop, Sara removed a well-worn pair, pulled them on her swollen feet and laced each up as best she could. Glancing out the window and checking the street as she normally did before she descended the stairs to walk back to Uncle Nels, Sara saw Dr. Harem's horse and cart outside his office. "Must have just come home from a house call. Wonder where he's been. Bet the nosey Mrs. Primrose knows. Wonder how Juliet has put up with her all this time. Juliet is a saint," declared Sara as she marched toward her shop door, shut it and made sure that it locked. The short walk took her across the bridge to the cabin she now called home.

Loud noises of men laughing greeted her as she reached the front door of Uncle Nels'. "Sounds like we have company. Hope they don't expect food. I'm too tired to cook and my feet are too sore to stand and do so. Glad I made those cookies. Should still be some left," came from Sara out of earshot of the others. Opening the door, Sara was shocked to see the man that she'd been so suspicious of who'd come off the west bound train sitting in Uncle Nels' favorite chair. It was impossible for her to sneak upstairs to her bedroom without being seen by those sitting near the fireplace. Sara set her shoes down on the rug by the door and walked over to the group. Alex was the first to react to her presence.

"Sara. You've finally left the shop. Wondered if I'd have to come over and escort you home. Look who's here. Sara, this is Clarence Alexanderson, my grandfather on my father's side."

Grateful that the threatening looking man was no longer someone needing to be careful around, Sara reached out her hand to shake his as he stood in greeting. "Your grandfather. The one you talked about earlier today? From your father's side, you said. When did you arrive from The Old Country, Mr. Alexanderson?"

Swedish words flew from Alex's mouth as he translated Sara's words. Sara watched Uncle Nels, wondering what his reaction would be, having a Swede in the house.

"Sorry. I'll need to translate for him as best I can. My Swedish isn't great but it will have to do. He's the last of his three siblings. The others have died over the last five years. Not wanting to be alone, he decided to find my father, unaware of his death. When he found my mother, she sent him to find me and here he is, surprised that I'm not in some logging camp up North."

"Does he intend to stay in this country?"

"Don't know Sara. Too soon to tell I'd think. Don't know where else he'd go."

Realizing she and Alex had made the man uncomfortable, Sara gestured that he sit. He willingly did, tired from his travel on the train, his spending time with Agnes, the lady whose basket he'd bought to stave his hunger, and the experience of finding his grandchild here in Goose. "Please, Alex, I know the three of you were enjoying each other's company before I came. I am tired and my feet hurt from those blessed shoes. I am going upstairs. I'll talk to you again tomorrow. I'll be up early tomorrow to make biscuits. Come before you go to the livery. Uncle Nels has some sorting out to do now that Nelson and the cattle are here. You'll need to know what his plans are too" and she turned and headed up the stairs.

25 Clarence

Nels walked to the livery stable with Alex once they had washed and cleaned up the leavings from breakfast the following morning. The two found Nelson feeding cattle and making sure there was water for them. The windmill was going, pumping water into the water trough, replenishing the water supply depleted by the cattle. Carrying water to the water troughs was not something Nelson was used to doing but knew had to be done to keep his cattle healthy. Reds were used to water available all the time. The run off streams from the Nordic mountains supplied what they needed. Seeing Alex first and then his father coming down the street, he stopped in the doorway of the livery and set his pails at his feet. He asked his far (father), "Decided when we should move the herd?"

"Let them rest a day or two. We'll need to find two or three more men willing to help us along the way. Farmers or homesteaders, whatever you want to call them, are not happy with any herds crossing their land. We'll need to keep the Reds together so that as little land as possible is disturbed by them even if harvest is over. The farmers are pretty particular about trails on the fields. Roads run west of here to the Red River. We'll follow them as much as possible and then head north when we reach the river."

"Been back there lately, Far?"

"No. Wish I had been better at checking on the place. It's been two years. The house was sturdy built. Only the barn needed a few shingles replaced. I made some spares and asked that they keep an eye on the roof. Promises were made to do so. The renters have just left so the buildings should be good."

"Know of any horses for sale?"

"Harmen has five, I think. His come from good stock. They are not like Stout at all, more a riding horse. Do you have penger to buy them?"

"Ja. I sold the rest of my herd before I came, taking only what I considered the best with me – the ones I thought could withstand the journey best." Pausing to think, Nelson scratched his whiskered chin and eyeing Alex continued. "Alex, will you come and take a look at them with me? I know so little about horses from this country. I wouldn't know what to look for."

"Sure if it's all right with you Nels. Let's go talk to Harem when you're finished with your chores, Nelson. See if he's going out to his land or not and is willing to show us his stock. I need to check on Pa (grandfather) over at the hotel before we leave. I'll come back here as soon as I can. You have a horse I can ride to Harem's?"

"Alex, you ride my roan. You've been on him before so he should not give you any trouble. Nelson, you take Stout. You have ridden him too. It's a long walk out to Harem's if you don't take a horse. I'll stay at the furniture store and put a sign on the door at noon so that I can check on Clarence for you, Alex.

"I'll let him know that I'll come and have a bowl of soup with him at the hotel tonight when I get back," decided Alex before he left the livery. "Coax him to talk. He can speak a little English. He is so embarrassed with his mispronunciation of some words that he pretends he doesn't know how."

Clarence hadn't come to the house for breakfast as invited. Glad for a single room with a decent bed that he didn't have to share with another man, he'd climbed the stairs, opened his door and walked to the window across from the door to his room. He stood a while checking the street below and found it empty. Marta's boarding house was filled when he went to ask about a room there, so he'd stayed at the hotel. For breakfast he'd eaten part of a loaf of bread he'd saved in his satchel and smeared on the slices the limburger cheese he'd bought at an earlier stop. The small villages like Goose Crossing surprised him as he'd crossed the country on his train ride from New York. He'd found all of the little communities he stopped at for an overnight and a good meal active during the day and sleepy at night. He sensed living in this country would be so different from the Scandinavian mountains of his homeland and the little "koping" he'd lived near all his life. The kopings back in Sweden were family settlements with as much of the daily needs it took to survive made, sold or shared within the family that lived close. Each person was responsible for his or her share of the work. From the little he'd seen of him, Alex, he'd decided, must have his father's traits, well disciplined, honest, and dependable. His mind's ramblings stopped when he heard heavy footsteps and then a knock on his door.

"Pa, are you awake? Eaten anything?"

Glad to open the door to a familiar voice, he did so and hugged the last living family relative. "You come for me? I had bread and cheese left that I bought somewhere along the way and didn't want to waste it so I ate here in this room."

"Didn't come for you but wanted to tell you where I'll be for a little while. Nelson needs to buy two horses and he doesn't know anything about American horses. He's asked me to help him. I'm going to ride out with him to where the horses are for sale and won't be back until this evening."

"Is there anything I can do to pass time?"

"Go to the train station. Rufus is a good soul and will spend time with you when he's not busy. So will Nels if he doesn't have anyone come to his furniture store. When I come back, we've been invited to Marta's to have supper."

"After that, can we come back here? I have news from home for you, Alex."

"That sounds good to me too. I know so little about my father's side of the family. Walk with me to the livery and I'll introduce you to Rufus." Clarence followed his grandson with a hesitancy in his step, unsure if he knew enough English words to talk to anyone for any length of time.

26 Case

Alex and Nelson returned to Goose as the sun settled in the western sky. Each had a paint trailing on a rope behind them. Harem was true to his word and did have five horses he was willing to sell and offered to let Nelson ride each. Taking his time, Nelson took each horse into a herd of cattle nearby and cut a single cow out of the bunch. Next, he asked each horse to back when he roped a yearling. All five responded well so Nelson took the two Alex considered the healthiest of the five and paid for them. Arriving at the stable, Alex handed his reins to Nelson, and headed for Marta's to clean up and change clothes before supper. Looking down the street, he saw his grandfather walking towards him so he waited. "Come sit in the porch swing while I clean up and change clothes. I know I smell cattle and Marta will not be happy if I come to supper in these clothes. Did you have a good day?"

"Rufus was kind enough to take me around town and introduce me to some of the shop keepers. I sat a time around the stove, pot belly I think you call it, and listened to the men talk. It helps me learn the English. You go. I'll wait here for you" and he sat in the swing to wait. Marta saw Alex enter to go to his room and stopped him. "Alex, have your grandfather come to the kitchen table. I have set out glasses of homemade dandelion wine. He can sip on that while you clean up. Leave those clothes you're wearing outside on the back porch, please, or you will smell up the whole upstairs. Shoes too!"

Alex turned around and went out on the front porch again, told his grandfather to go to the kitchen and went around the house to the back door. Removing his shoes and pants, he hoped that the lady renters were not around. As quickly as he could, he made his way up the back stairs to his room. Marta had been thoughtful once again. The pitcher on the washstand in his room was full of tepid water waiting for him to use. He poured the basin full, took the soap from its dish and began to scrub with the washcloth that hung at ready. Drying himself with the bath towel, he donned a clean pair of underwear, socks, shirt and pants. The only other pair of shoes he had was his Sunday shoes. Slipping them on, he spiffed up his hair and made his way down and into the kitchen and saw that others had joined his grandfather. "Nels, Sara, good to see you. Nelson tell you we found two good paints?"

"He did," answered Nels. "He'll be along as soon as he has them settled in the livery."

"Say prayers, Nels. The venison steaks are ready. We won't wait for Nelson. He'll have to eat when he gets here. What a treat the fresh venison will be thanks to you, Nels." Prayers said, the four made their way to the sideboard in the dining area and filled plates. "I've made mushroom gravy for the steaks. Helps to tenderize them. Save room for cake."

Little was said around the table. Each enjoyed the meal, relishing the mashed potatoes with mushroom gravy. Baking the steaks in the mushroom gravy gave them a special flavor. Meal finished, Clarence was the first to offer to help clear the table. Alex who didn't ever remember his father doing any woman's work registered surprise. "Tonight we help you. Thanks for a good meal. We'll bring you dishes. You wash, I wipe," he declared.

"When we're done, I need to go back to the shop and finish Mrs. Primrose's latest order. I have the hem in a skirt left, Uncle Nels. Should take about an hour or so. Then I'll come home."

"I've promised grandfather I'd just sit and talk with him. We haven't had a chance to do that since he came," said Alex.

"That'll leave you and me, Marta. Will you sit on the porch and swing with me?"

"Thought you'd never ask," came from Marta with a smile meant only for Nels.

When the kitchen chores were finished, Alex walked next door to the hotel with his grandfather, conscious of the elderly man's unsteady gate and tiredness. Entering, Clarence said, "Let's find a quiet spot in the dining room. Have some coffee. I have lots to tell you, Alex."

"Pa Clarence, are you well? You seem more tired tonight than I have seen you," said Alex as he helped his grandfather off with his overcoat and placed it on an extra chair beside him.

Tonight is not a good night for me. I have spells of not feeling well. I suppose it is my heart. With your father gone, you and I are all that are left of our family besides your mother. I have seen that she will not have to work the rest of her life. All of the lands and mine are left to me when my brothers all died. Taking his coat, he pulled out an envelope from the inside pocket. I hope you will be interested in my proposal, my grandson. None of us know how much time we have left to live."

"Would you like to see Doctor Harem? I'm sure he'd see you tonight if you don't feel well." Alex noticed that his English was so much better when the two of them were alone.

"No, a little sleep and I will be better in the morning." The coffee came and the two laced their cups with cream and sugar. "Before I went to visit your mother, I spent some time in Wisconsin looking for your father. Our last contact with him was a letter sent to me just before he joined the army. The army people told me he'd moved to St. Paul and that is where I finally found your mother. I have been reading as best I can about the Bonanza farmers and the large acreage that they work on those farms. Most are still using horses, I understand. The J. I. Case Company in Wisconsin is making a steam tractor."

"I have not heard about the tractor. Have you seen one?"

"I saw it working in a field when I went there. It can do ten times the work in an hour that a horse drawn piece of equipment can do. I visited the Case Company and arranged to talk to Mr. Case. He has agreed to supply tractors for you to sell."

"What do you mean by sell? How will that be good for me?" asked Alex, concerned about having some money to live on.

"He will sell them to you a little above cost. You sell them for whatever price you think you can get for

them. This is what the machine looks like." He took out a postcard with a picture of the steam tractor.
"The men in the lumber camps could use it too. It's a good idea for the farmers and for the wood cutters, but how can I sell something I don't even know how to run, Pa?"
"His company holds a school where you go and learn how to run the machines with engines."
"Engines?"
"The engines are from 9hp to 150hp. The steam pressure in the gas run boiler is what generates the horse power. Anyone buying a tractor would have to go to a school too."
"I'd have to demonstrate how it works."
"You would. Once they see how much quicker the work can be done, you will have no trouble selling the tractor."
"How much can the biggest one pull, Pa?"
"The 150 horsepower Case is called the Road Locomotive. I saw it pull 30 plow bottoms. It can pull more if the soil conditions are good. The smaller one can pull a six bottom plow."

"No wonder the work gets done faster than using horses. I'd need a good sized store front to have three or four different sizes of the machines on display and a place out back to demonstrate."
"We could buy land just outside of Goose. While you're at school learning to run the machines, the building could be constructed."
"I have a little money set aside from my carving. I'd have to talk to Lucas and see if he would let me borrow the rest."
"Money is not a problem. I sold the mine just before I came. Here, Alex, read this." Clarence handed Alex another envelope. Inside was a will. Alex read:

To whom it may concern:
 I, Clarence Alexanderson, leave all of my fortune to Alex Alexanderson, the last living male relative in my family. The money has been transferred to Goose Bank, Goose Crossing, Minnesota. My only wish is that I may live the rest of my life close to him as he lives his life.
 (signed) Clarence Alexanderson

Tears rolled down Alex's face. He stood and hugged his grandfather, overwhelmed with the generosity of the old man.
"Think overnight about becoming a tractor salesman. We'll go see Lucas in the morning and talk about what needs to be done to get your name on the banking papers and the money transferred. If the steam engine tractor is not something that interests you, we'll find something else. You have a good head on your shoulders, Alex." He rubbed his forehead and continued. "I need the rest. We'll meet in the morning.

Come when you are free." Clarence rose with difficulty, put his coat over his shoulder and slowly climbed the stairs to his room.

Alex rose behind him, went to the desk and paid Carl for the coffees. Once outside the hotel, he walked towards the river and sat on the bluff rock, needing time. Could he sell tractors? Could he learn to run them well enough to teach others to run them? What would Nels do for a carver if he left? And Sara? Would she decide to stay? He knew the dress shop was given to her. He'd thought about asking her to marry him. Would she be happy with him gone off to school or training others to run the tractors? Maybe he wouldn't have to be gone so much. Maybe he could train a crew of men to take a tractor out like Nels does his McCormick binder. The position of the moon told him it was very late. He rose and did the only thing he knew to do when he was troubled. He prayed for guidance and answers to tomorrow's questions, knowing that his decisions would affect many lives.

Synopsis of Historical Fiction books written by Jan Smith:

America Bound
The Journey West 1790

Bjorn, eighteen and considered an adult by Nordic mountain standards, seeks his fortune in the New World in 1790. His adventure of working his way on a raft, a three-masted schooner, and as a scout on an oxcart and wagon train place him in unfamiliar and exciting situations as he pursues his dream of seeking his fortune along the Red River of the North in the Northwest Territories labeled the Land of Milk and Honey.

199 pages - author illustrated

Homesteading the Land
Phelps Mill 1890

The story is set in Otter Tail County in the **Phelps Mill** area known then as Maine, Minnesota. Arriving by prairie schooner, living in a tent, building a sod house and finally a log home, each become adventures for Nivek. Almost daily visits to the mill delivering lunch, to McConkey's store, school and farming, fishing and hunting (sometimes with the neighbor boys) become "lessons in life." **Homesteading the Land** is a fictional look at the daily life of a land-claiming family of five in the year 1890. Many of the characters, events and places, however, allude to *actual local people and happenings* of that year.

197 pages – author illustrated

Remembering the Maine
Riding with Roosevelt - 1898

Remembering the Maine continues the story of the young Nivek James, introduced in the previous book **Homesteading the Land**. Leaving his family homestead in Minnesota, he becomes a newspaper correspondent during the Spanish-American War, 1898. With his boyhood friends, Wing, an Ojibwa Indian, and Jesse, from Medora, North Dakota, the young men travel across country by horseback, train, and stagecoach on their journey to join the Rough Riders and Theodore Roosevelt. This book is the story of their journey, the training of the troops, and the war in Cuba. It is a coming-of-age tale of bravery, courage, hardships and patriotism set against the background of emergence of the U.S.A. as a world power. Nivek's dispatches to the **Minnesota News** give a personal account of the times.

201 pages - author illustrated

Synopsis of Troll Tales books written by Jan Smith

Jan's storytelling at many Nordic events spurred the writing of the Troll Series. Her tales intersperse factual Nordic and North American geology with a mythological explanation of how the New World became populated with a diversity of people.

Crossing the Arctic   A Norse Fjell Troll Story

Crossing the Arctic is the story of a Norse Fjell Trollet, a mountain troll. Ridiculed because of his lack of cleanliness, Fy decides to follow in his father's footsteps and make his way from Norway to the **New World** in order to start a new life for himself. Receded fjord waters impacted by glacial movement and ice jams in the Arctic allow Fy to take advantage of his huge height and *walk* across. Two Nisse, small Norse troll people, accompany him and the three face adventures on the journey to the **New World**.

Fy and Aina   A New World Love Story

Fy and Aina continues the story of the first book in the Norse Trollology Series **Crossing the Arctic**. This second book begins with Fy from his mountain cave close to the ocean hearing plaintive cries for Hjelpe (help)! The story finds Fy struggling with loneliness, performing a water rescue, searching for a soul mate, and grappling with the hardships of living in an untamed New World. It is a look at what can happen if people of two opposite cultures like the Fjell trolls and the Nisse, who are small dwarf like trolls, have compassions for the other's life.

Place order for books on
Amazon.com

CONTACT AUTHOR
website: jansmithwriter.com

Made in the USA
Lexington, KY
15 September 2017